"You're better off without him," said Luciano.

"Yes, I am. It put me off the notion of men altogether," replied Sophie.

"And now?"

"I'm coming around to the idea again." Was it her imagination or were they flirting during this little heart-to-heart? She was afraid to call it that, but there was definitely something springing to life between them.

"I know what you mean. It was different with my wife and I. There was no cheating or Vegas wedding involved, but I didn't think there'd be anyone after her."

"And now?"

"I'm coming around to the idea." His coy smile was as intoxicating as the wine she was sipping.

Dear Reader,

As I write this, I think most of us are missing our holidays in the sun and the freedom to travel. I had no idea when I was writing this book that the world would end up being such a different place to the one we take for granted.

Hopefully, Sophie's travels around the Mediterranean with her hunky Italian doctor will help you escape for a while and serve as a reminder of those places we can visit again someday in the future.

Stay safe.

Karin xx

ONE NIGHT WITH HER ITALIAN DOC

―

KARIN BAINE

**MEDICAL
ROMANCE**

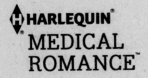

HARLEQUIN®
MEDICAL
ROMANCE™

Recycling programs
for this product may
not exist in your area.

ISBN-13: 978-1-335-40426-8

One Night with Her Italian Doc

Copyright © 2020 by Karin Baine

This edition published by arrangement with Harlequin Books S.A.

For questions and comments about the quality of this book,
please contact us at CustomerService@Harlequin.com.

Harlequin Enterprises ULC
22 Adelaide St. West, 40th Floor
Toronto, Ontario M5H 4E3, Canada
www.Harlequin.com

Printed in U.S.A.

For D xx

**Praise for
Karin Baine**

"Karin Baine is a phenomenally talented writer of contemporary romances who writes books that are so poignant and well-written that they never fail to tug at the heartstrings…. *Midwife Under the Mistletoe* is a searingly emotional Medical Romance that is powerfully written, wonderfully emotional and absolutely breathtaking."

Karin Baine lives in Northern Ireland with her husband, two sons and her out-of-control notebook collection. Her mother and her grandmother's vast collection of books inspired her love of reading and her dream of becoming a Harlequin author. Now she can tell people she has a *proper* job! You can follow Karin on Twitter, @karinbaine1, or visit her website for the latest news—karinbaine.com.

Books by Karin Baine

Harlequin Medical Romance

Pups that Make Miracles

Their One-Night Christmas Gift

Single Dad Docs

The Single Dad's Proposal

Paddington Children's Hospital

Falling for the Foster Mom

Reforming the Playboy
Their Mistletoe Baby
From Fling to Wedding Ring
Midwife Under the Mistletoe
Their One-Night Twin Surprise
Healed by Their Unexpected Family
Reunion with His Surgeon Princess

Visit the Author Profile page
at Harlequin.com for more titles.

CHAPTER ONE

SOPHIE BLYTHE WAS a terrible, horrible person. Why else would the woman she'd agreed to care for on the cruise of a lifetime currently be on a drip in the onboard medical centre?

'I'm so sorry, Edith. It's my fault you're in this state. I should've been keeping a closer eye on you.'

'Nonsense. I'm seventy-eight years old. I'm responsible for my own actions,' she insisted, albeit weakly, from her hospital bed.

'You brought me with you on this trip to look after you.' So far, she hadn't done a very good job. They'd only boarded the cruise ship at Barcelona three days ago and they were already having a medical emergency.

Working full time in a care home, it was literally Sophie's job to look after the elderly and infirm. She had only taken time out because her neighbour had asked her to accompany her on this trip. With her mobility issues, Edith needed someone to help her get around and Sophie had been keen to escape from the aftermath of her break-up with Ryan. A cruise around the Mediterranean was supposed to be doing them both a world of good. But they were off to a dubious start.

Edith slid her hand over the crisp white sheets to clasp Sophie's. 'You've been a blessing to me. I wouldn't have seen half of the things so far if it hadn't been for you taking care of me and organising transportation. It's not your fault this silly old woman fell asleep on her balcony in the sun. Stop worrying.'

The reminder of those adventures they'd enjoyed before her travel companion had become ill raised a smile on Sophie's lips. They'd been overawed by the sheer volume of noise and number of people in Barcelona as they'd explored the sprawling stalls of Las Ramblas, looking for souvenirs.

Later, the hop-on-hop-off bus they'd taken at their leisure had driven past all manner of designer stores and the fantasy-scape of Gaudi's architecture. She'd found joy in the chatter of the parakeets high up in the trees and the sight of decorative water imps playing in the majestic fountains before they'd even embarked on the ship.

'Pompeii was certainly an experience, wasn't it?' They'd wandered the sprawling ruins of Pompeii together, both amazed at the mosaics and painting still visible in some of the buildings, and solemn when they'd seen the body casts of those frozen in time by the eruption of Vesuvius.

'It was. Naples wasn't at all what I expected either. So many colourful scooters and those Italian policemen…phew.' Edith's sense of humour had helped make this trip so much fun and had taken Sophie's mind off matters at home in England.

Waking up in the mornings in her state room, opening the curtains to find herself in a different port every day was exactly the kind of adventure Sophie thought she needed to re-centre herself.

This Bohemian lifestyle suited her. She'd lived it in her twenties. Once she'd got her nursing qualifications, she'd travelled the world, using her skills to take placements where she could. It was a legacy from her parents that she hadn't been able to stay still for long. Her father had been a wannabe rock star who'd had no intention of giving up touring pubs and clubs simply because he'd got someone pregnant.

He hadn't put her mother off unsuitable men either. He was only one in a line of eternal bachelors she'd followed from town to town, hopping from one relationship to the next in the hope of finding love. They were hardly the foundations for a stable childhood. Or role models. Sophie had no experience of settled family life. She didn't even know where either of them were at this moment in time.

If it hadn't been for Ryan she might still be flitting from one city to the next, but she'd fallen head over heels for him when they'd met in Thailand. He'd convinced her to go back with him to England and settle down. It was everything you were supposed to do for someone you loved. Yet it was a decision she'd come to regret. Domestic life had squashed her free spirit and left her trapped in a semi-detached in Kent. Perhaps she was more like her father with the wandering feet than she'd thought.

Ryan had simply wanted a normal life and she'd tried to be the partner to share it with him. They had loved each other back then. She simply hadn't realised that the adventurous spirit she'd seen in him in Phuket had been a one-time deal. It had meant giving up travelling in exchange for a mortgage and a permanent job in the countryside, too far from London and the city life she'd grown up in for her restless spirit.

After three years together she'd told him how trapped she felt and had pushed for something to inject some excitement into their relationship. When he'd agreed that their relationship had grown stale, she'd imagined swapping suburbia for a trek in the Himalayas or kayaking in Patagonia.

Ryan had taken it to mean he should run off with his co-worker at the bank, to get married in Las Vegas, leaving Sophie with a life she'd never wanted. He was being 'true to his heart,' apparently. She had no idea how long Ryan had been sleeping with his colleague before he'd decided he wanted to be with her for ever, but it had been less time than Sophie had wasted being with him. Now, with her spirit crushed, she didn't know what to do or where to go.

Thank goodness Edith had taken pity on her and flung her a lifeline. She'd suspected the generous offer had been more for her benefit than her dear neighbour's when she'd been so miserable. It was a shame this was how she'd repaid her kindness.

'I'll be back on my feet in no time,' she reassured Sophie.

'You'd better be. It's Rome next on the itinerary. We've still got to tick the Colosseum and the Trevi Fountain off your…list.' Sophie stopped before the word 'bucket' inserted itself in there. This was supposed to be Edith's 'last hurrah before she croaked.' Her words, not Sophie's.

She'd wanted to see Italy and France one final time before she was no longer able to travel at all. Now those plans were in jeopardy and Sophie couldn't help but shower herself in blame.

'I'll still be able to do all that, won't I, Doctor?' Edith addressed the medic overseeing her treatment.

Sophie had been in so much of a panic when they'd first entered the clinic she hadn't given her attention to anyone other than Edith. Her friend had been whisked off for a series of tests, leaving Sophie to marinate in worry out at Reception. Now she could see why the other staff members had a twinkle in their eyes every time someone mentioned his name.

Dr Luciano Montavano was Italian, according to the flag on the badge pinned to his natty uniform. It was the only way she

would have known he was a doctor at all.
Dressed in his whites he looked like every
other officer she'd seen on board. Only much
more appealing to the eye than all the rest.

Sophie didn't have a particular type, finding herself more drawn to the soul within the
outer shell of a man. Although her judgement clearly needed some work in that department, none of that meant she couldn't
appreciate a handsome face or a to-die-for
body.

At five foot nine she was no slouch in
the height stakes, but he towered over her.
He was lean and tanned and his hair was
the same almost-black as his eyes, save for
the few strands of silver streaking his tem-
ples. It was as if the cruise company had
drafted him in especially so the passengers
had something good to look at whilst they
were at sea.

Sophie tutted, disgusted with herself for
being so easily distracted by such a shallow
thing as someone's appearance and focused
back on Edith, who was enduring the ship's
nurse's repeated attempts to insert a cannula
into her arm.

'Would you like me to do that? I'm a qualified nurse.' She grimaced at the harsh tone
of her own voice but Edith had been through

so much already it didn't seem fair to keep pricking her with needles.

'So am I. Thank you,' the nurse with the American twang said through a forced smile and gritted teeth.

'Mrs Fields is very dehydrated after the vomiting. It makes it difficult to find a suitable vein,' the Italian distraction informed her.

She knew that, of course she did, but she wanted to do something useful. After all, she hadn't been there during the night when Edith had needed her most. If only she'd knocked on the wall or shouted for her, Sophie could have done something or gone for help sooner. Instead, Edith had decided not to bother anyone and had been ill all through the night alone, until Sophie had called to take her to breakfast.

'There we are.' The American in blue scrubs eventually managed to get a line in and shot her a triumphant look.

'I want a saline drip and we'll do some more scans when she's rehydrated.' Dr Montavano consulted his next in command quietly with Sophie straining to hear the conversation. She didn't appreciate being shut out when she'd told them she was a fellow professional, along with being Edith's carer.

'Have you checked her blood sugar?' Her question was directed at the doctor himself. She knew the standard protocols and wanted to make sure they were following them here. They might be on a ship in the middle of the sea but she still expected Edith to have the same healthcare she would receive anywhere else.

'Yes.' He sounded exasperated with her. Tough. She would make a nuisance of herself until she was sure Edith was in better hands than hers.

'What about her sodium, electrolytes and kidney function? Do you even have the lab facilities to do all that here?'

'We're monitoring Mrs Fields as best we can.'

'I'm not sure that's good enough.' Not that they had any other choice at present but at least by making her professional status known they wouldn't be able to fob Edith off with anything less than the best treatment available.

'Sophie, everyone has been very attentive. Please, don't worry.' Edith tried to put her mind at rest but it was only natural to be concerned when they were so far from home and the medical services they took for granted.

'As long as you're okay, that's all that matters.' She didn't want to upset Edith, so she'd simply have to bite her tongue and let the others get on with their work. It didn't mean she wouldn't be keeping a close eye on things, though.

'Will I have to stay here overnight, Doctor?'

'I'm afraid so, Mrs Fields.' That accent was too much. Surely he was over-egging it? He probably did this with all the female tourists to give them a thrill.

'We want to watch you.'

Sophie snorted. 'I'll stay with you, Edith, while you're here under *observation*,' she said, correcting the doctor's unfortunate phrasing.

'I'm afraid that won't be possible Ms...' He stood with his hands clasped behind his back, waiting for her to introduce herself.

'Blythe. Sophie Blythe.'

'Sophie.' He tested her name on his lips and gave her a cheek-reddening smile.

This was ridiculous.

'I'm afraid we do not have the space to accommodate you.'

'I'll just stay here.' She plonked herself into the unyielding plastic chair by the bed.

It wasn't as though she would take up too much room.

A frown marked the doctor's otherwise perfect features. 'We can only let you come here during visiting hours. As you can see, we are a small facility. We might need this room to accommodate emergencies.'

'I would've thought this constituted an emergency.'

A bell rang out down the corridor.

'That's the end of visiting, I'm afraid.' The nurse didn't bother turning around to glance at Sophie and carried on hooking up Edith's drip. She didn't have to when Sophie knew she'd be sporting a look of relief, glad to get rid of her. If their roles were reversed she wouldn't be happy with someone trying to tell her how to do her job either.

'When can I come back?' She didn't want to whine or appear petulant but Edith had paid a lot of money for Sophie to be with her. If only they hadn't had separate cabins she might have been saved from all of this. As it was, all Sophie could do was keep her company during her treatment.

'Next visiting is from three p.m. to six p.m.' He positioned his hand in the small of her back and gently tried to guide her out the door.

Sophie dug her heels in. 'Wait. Are you actually throwing me out?'

His grin tempted her to stamp hard on his foot. 'Visiting is at three p.m.'

'What am I supposed to do until then?'

'Lie by the pool, drink cocktails, go dancing and do all the things I wish I could do. You're young. Go and enjoy yourself.' Edith waved a hand at her as she ganged up with the others and dismissed her from her duties.

'Your grandmother is right.'

Sophie rolled her eyes as her medical credentials were sidelined for a narrative that suited him better.

'Edith is not my grandmother.'

'Go, enjoy your vacation.'

'I'm not on vacation,' she protested as he propelled her out the door and down the corridor.

'Miss… Sophie, your…friend needs lots of rest. You, however, seem as though you need to cut loose for a while. There is free food and free drink available. You could take in a show while you wait. There is no need to worry. Mrs Fields is in good hands.' Those same hands guided her through Reception, leaving Sophie spluttering with indignation as he closed the door on her.

'I'll be back,' she shouted through the

closed door before she realised it sounded like a threat. 'For visiting. Later.'

There was no reply. She tried the door one last time but they'd closed up shop. The note taped to the wall advised that visitors were required to phone ahead to gain access outside the approved hours, something she didn't think the officious doctor would be in a hurry to do.

The long corridor was empty apart from the vending machine that dispensed basic medical necessities such as sticking plasters and antiseptic for those unfortunate enough to hurt themselves out of hours. It struck her how quiet it was at this end of the ship. A conscious design decision, she supposed, for the patients to find some peace away from the partying. However, it meant there was simply nothing for her to do here until she was able to check on Edith again. There wasn't even a seat to sit on.

She walked farther into the belly of the ship, exchanging greetings with the stewards scurrying in and out of the cabins, who were getting them spotless again before the guests returned from their leisure pursuits.

The lifts were busy transporting guests to the many decks, so Sophie took the stairs instead. Happy families and couples dressed for the pool or a spot of sunbathing stepped in time beside her and she followed them out onto the top deck.

She blinked as she emerged into the sunlight, feeling the heat immediately kissing her bare skin. Her senses kicked in all at once, assaulted by the noise of the loud music, the sight of the crowds dancing and the smell of chlorine, sun cream and food. She hadn't realised there was an all-day buffet provided. It reminded her of a school cafeteria, only with better quality food. Edith preferred to sit in one of the more civilised restaurants downstairs. Sophie's stomach rumbled, letting her know it wasn't fussy and she was yet to have lunch.

Perhaps she'd avail herself of one of the sun loungers lining the deck and enjoy an al fresco snack with everyone else. She might even indulge in one of those delicious-looking frozen cocktails in plentiful supply. It was just the thing to take the edge off the day's drama and it might even help her forget Deliciano Luciano, who'd managed to get her adrenaline pumping without even trying.

Luciano watched as the door rattled with Miss Blythe still ranting on the other side of it, a smirk playing on his lips. But it was soon followed by a frown. He shouldn't be amused or find this Sophie person intriguing. For eight months at sea, in his new role as cruise doctor, he'd managed to keep that professional line drawn between him and the passengers and he preferred to keep it that way.

He turned away, hotfooting it back to his patient and the safety of the treatment rooms.

'Sorry about that, Mrs Fields. Now, we will let the drip do its work and take another look at you later.'

'Yes, Doctor.'

That was what he liked. A compliant patient. Sometimes they had to deal with people who'd overindulged in the unlimited alcohol, but if they were too raucous, Security got involved. In extreme cases they'd be ejected from the ship, holiday over. He didn't get a lot of dissension in his own little kingdom here. Certainly, he wasn't used to fellow medical professionals challenging him or his authority. As a result, he was finding it difficult to shift thoughts of the rebellious Sophie out of his head.

'I'm sure you're glad to see the back of her. Wowee,' Patrice, the nurse who'd witnessed most of their exchange, whispered as they left the room.

'She's clearly very concerned.' He didn't want to make excuses for her but neither did he wish to bad-mouth her in her absence. In the past, he too had demanded the right to be included in a loved one's treatment. Many times, in fact.

Each time Renata had lost one of their precious babies, and finally when she'd contracted sepsis, he'd been there, taking out his pain on the very people trying to help his wife. He should have known better and had always apologised after the fact but it helped him understand Sophie's frustrations. What he was struggling to figure out was his reaction to her. Since Renata, he hadn't so much as looked at another woman, never mind given anyone a second thought. Much to his mother's despair.

'You're my handsome boy, Luciano. I know you loved Renata very much. We all did. But you deserve to be happy again,' she'd said to him before he'd left. What she'd meant was that he deserved to have another chance at having a family. Her desire for more grandchildren was no doubt behind the determination to see him married again.

He felt the pressure to meet someone new, despite it being only two years since he'd lost his wife, because his parents' marriage was held up as a template for the rest of the family. They'd been childhood sweethearts, had married young and raised four children—all whilst tending their own vineyard. It was a recipe for a good life that he and his siblings had all wanted to replicate.

He was the only one to have failed so far. Even his kid brother had got engaged and now the expectation weighing down on Luciano had become suffocating. It was even more painful because his own house had become so lonely and empty without Renata waiting for him there. She'd been stolen away from him too soon, along with the dream of having a family of their own.

That was why he'd given up his role as a family practitioner and signed on for the life of a cruise doctor—where relationships amongst the crew were frowned on and he was able to hide out in the medical centre. Working and sleeping was how he spent his days and nights, and he'd been content to do so, foregoing the crew social scene and excursions ashore. He was simply trundling along, existing without having to deal with real life outside. He didn't want anyone else. Not when it meant suffering that same crushing pain when they vanished from existence. He'd barely survived losing the wife and babies who'd been everything to him. There wouldn't be a second time.

It suited him to drift along with the tide, not under any pressure to find another significant other. Something he'd done happily for the entirety of his contract so far. So why, after a brief, emotionally charged introduction to one particular guest, could he remember every single detail of it? And her? Her long dark hair, her sparkling blue eyes and the freckles on her bare shoulders where the sun had been lucky enough to touch her skin.

It was unsettling to be jolted out of this safe space he'd created for himself onboard the ship. Therefore, Mrs Fields and her companion would become his top priority. Then he could discharge them both and let them get back to their holiday whilst he returned to his usual, solitary routine.

CHAPTER TWO

IN THE GOOD old days, Sophie wouldn't have thought twice about lying by the pool, knocking back luminous alcoholic drinks.

That had been pre-Ryan. Since then she'd realised the importance of responsibility and the consequences of people shirking. It made her think twice about taking off into the great unknown again, unprepared with no back-up plan if things fell through. He'd been a valuable lesson to someone who'd thought she'd achieved what her parents couldn't by settling down with one person for the rest of her life. Not so useful to a person trying to relax. Thanks to him, she was no longer able to switch off that part of her brain that worried about poor Edith lying in a hospital bed.

'Your drink, ma'am.' A waiter—Carlo, according to his name badge—appeared by her side and extended a tray towards her.

'Oh, thank you.' Despite her reticence, Sophie had decided to take Edith's advice and at least try to enjoy herself. And she was starting by taking advantage of the all-inclusive drinks package.

'You know we have a singles club for passengers travelling on their own. I think they're hosting a getting-to-know-each-other disco tonight. There's no need to sit up here on your own. There are plenty of other singletons on board you could meet up with.' The earnest waiter was being so super-friendly she was trying not to take offence, despite the fact that he was only a few years younger than she was and clearly thought she was some charity case desperately in need of friends.

'That's okay. I'm not—'

'No need to be ashamed. Everyone's a bit nervous at first but, believe me, by the end of this cruise you'll be having the time of your life.'

What could she do but smile sweetly and sip her drink, hoping it would extinguish the indignant fire burning in her belly. It wasn't Carlo's fault he'd touched on an exposed nerve. Even she hadn't realised the break-up was still affecting her. It wasn't that she was missing Ryan, but seeing everyone else coupled up and enjoying their holiday was a constant reminder that she was on her own. In her early twenties she'd had the world at her feet. She'd been unafraid to go it alone. She wished she could get that person back.

'Is there anything else I can get for you?'

An invisibility cloak?

The attentive Carlo was waiting for further instruction and she wondered how many lonely women propositioned him during their holiday. More to the point, how many he actually obliged.

'No, thank you. I have everything I need.' She raised her glass, which was full of Irish liqueur, vodka, ice cream and chocolate sauce. It was more dessert than drink but calling it a cocktail apparently lessened its calorific content.

Once she was on her own again she was able to relax more. There was a fiesta vibe as the DJ cranked up the music and people were strutting their stuff on the open-air dance floor.

Sophie unfastened her halter-neck top and slid her shorts off to take in the sun's rays along with everyone else, grateful she had packed a couple of bikinis at the last minute. She popped on her sunglasses, lowered the back on her lounger and stretched out.

With her ice-cream cocktail and the plate of food she'd helped herself to from the buffet, she was all set for the afternoon. It wasn't long before her earlier stress began to ebb away and the encounter with Dr Montavano seemed like a bad dream.

'Ahem.'

Sophie was woken up some time later by someone clearing their throat nearby. It was easy to see how Edith had dozed off in the heat, with the gentle motion of the ship rocking her to sleep like a baby in a crib. Thankfully Sophie had had the foresight to put on sunscreen before getting dressed this morning to avoid suffering as Edith had.

She stretched her arms out over the top of the sun bed with a yawn. Apparently, she was capable of chilling out after all. Perhaps it was a muscle memory left over from her more selfish, less responsible travelling years.

'Ahem.'

The throat-clearing sounded closer now as a large shadow settled over her, blocking out the sun. She took off her shades to get a better look at whoever was trying to get her attention. It was possible the everattentive Carlo was already trying to matchmake between his sad, lonely customers. She was going to have to be more forceful about not participating in any group activities. She wasn't on some booze cruise, where being on her own for five minutes was an invitation to any predatory males who happened by.

'I'm sorry but I would really appreciate being left alone. I've just got out of a soul-destroying relationship and the only love affair I'm interested in is one with myself.' It might sound egotistical, or like she was over-sharing, to someone she didn't know very well, but in her experience being polite in these situations didn't get the point across.

'That's good to know and I'm sorry to disturb your...self-love but I need to speak to you.'

She recognised that heavily accented voice and clumsy choice of words.

Once he stepped directly out of the sun, she could see it was the dishy Italian doctor she'd sparred with earlier.

'Sorry. I didn't realise it was you, Doctor. I had an attentive waiter trying to make me join the lonely hearts club.' Every word she'd uttered came back to haunt her. What must he think of her? Whatever it was had clearly amused him as she witnessed his attempt to hide a smirk.

'We did try to reach you in your cabin.'

'Everyone kept telling me to go and relax, so I did.' As she tried to justify her actions she began to pull on her shorts, aware she was lying here with only a few scraps of canary-yellow fabric to cover her modesty.

'Mrs Fields is experiencing some complications.' His face was deadly serious now, making Sophie's heart pound so hard in her ears it was deafening.

'What's happened? Is Edith okay?' She tugged her top on over her head, ready to move at a moment's notice.

'She's fine but I'd appreciate it if you'd could come with me back to the clinic to discuss her treatment.' He looked as uncomfortable as she felt fumbling with the straps of her halter-neck.

'Let me.'

Before she could protest, his warm hands brushed the sensitive skin of her neck to tie the ends of the coral-coloured straps securely.

'Thanks,' she croaked, her throat suddenly dry and her skin burning where his fingers had briefly made contact.

'It's not too tight?'

'No. Thank you.' She couldn't look at him. At least not until she'd stopped blushing.

Gathering up her belongings, she kept her back to him until she could trust herself not to make eye contact with the owner of those strong, confident hands.

Her thoughts were on Edith and what on earth had happened, but there was a small place taken up by reflecting on the effect the doctor was having on her. Perhaps Carlo was right and she'd been on her own too long.

Luciano was feeling the heat and not solely because he was standing in the sun in full uniform. He almost never ventured up on deck, especially not with the passengers. Neither did he usually volunteer to personally locate a family member. They could have made a public announcement over the loudspeaker to find her but, no, he'd insisted on breaking the news himself. Goodness knew why. She wasn't going to take it well. In fact, she'd probably vent her ire at him when he was the one who'd forced her out of the medical centre.

He was accepting responsibility for that decision and whatever Ms Sophie had to say on the matter.

If that was the sole truth he wouldn't be sweating now at the sight of her teeny-weeny two-piece. Neither would he have jumped at the chance to help cover her up, making skin-to-skin contact in the process.

He was at a loss to explain why he was acting like a nervous suitor around this particular passenger, who was a burst of sunshine yellow in his otherwise cloudy morning. Not only was he a doctor with considerable experience of dealing with the human body but pretty women of all ages and sizes came through the clinic and he'd barely noticed them beyond their ailments. Sophie had clearly rattled him by not falling into line earlier and this was him battling to regain some sort of control of the situation.

He watched and waited as she rolled up her towel, popped it into her bag and slipped her feet into her sandals. 'Okay, let's go.'

With a brief nod he took his cue to leave, heading towards the lift with Sophie falling in behind him.

'*Buenos días.*'

'*Bonjour, Capitaine.*'

'Hello, there.'

As they waited for the lift, Luciano was greeted by guests of all nationalities. He offered them all a '*Buongiorno*' in return.

'*Capitaine?*' Sophie mocked with a raised eyebrow.

He kept his eyes on the electronic display,

watching the numbers rise steadily towards their deck. Too slowly for his liking.

'It's the uniform. Happens all the time.'

'And, of course, you don't correct them.'

He jabbed the button again, even though it wasn't going to make the lift come any faster.

'I did for a while. The uniform confuses people and I don't like to embarrass them by correcting them when they're simply saying hello.' She didn't need to know about the selfies passengers demanded. They didn't care. All they wanted was a souvenir snap of a man in uniform and it was part of the reason he tried to avoid coming up here.

As soon as the lift door opened and the new batch of sun worshippers trooped out, Luciano stepped in. He only waited long enough for Sophie to join him before punching in the number for the clinic deck, hopefully before anyone else jumped in with them and forced small talk.

'What's happened to Edith? It must've been serious for *you* to come all this way to find me.' There was nowhere in this steel box to escape Sophie's scrutiny, or her temper if it got the better of her again.

It didn't matter about their personality clash to this point, it was his duty to be professional. He had hoped she'd wait until they got back to the clinic before he the news. At least there he had a sense of authority.

'I wanted to apologise for being so abrupt with you earlier. I understand you have a personal and professional investment in the patient.'

'Edith.'

'Edith. Although we were able to give her fluids and rehydrate her, her blood pressure remains high.'

'That's not unusual after being dehydrated, is it?'

Again, Sophie displayed her medical knowledge of the situation. With cases of dehydration the hormone vasopressin could be secreted into the bloodstream if sodium levels dropped as a result of losing too much fluid. Excess vasopressin could cause the blood vessels to constrict, thereby increasing blood pressure. He'd seen a lot of it over these past months. That was why he'd known something wasn't quite right here.

'No, but with her age I don't want to take any chances. We'll continue to monitor her.'

'But if you can't get it under control there's a chance it could lead to something more serious, such as a heart attack or stroke. This is exactly what I was worried about. I knew

I should've stayed with her but, oh, no, you knew best…' Unlike every other tourist he encountered, she wasn't impressed by his uniform or intimidated by his position. She drew herself up to her full height. Tall enough to be a model but still some way from his six-foot-two frame. She made for a worthy opponent, even though they were supposed to be on the same team.

'You can't do any more for her than we already have.'

'I should've stayed with her instead of swanning about the ship like I'm on holiday.' Beyond the anger as she squared up to him, Luciano could see guilty tears welling in her eyes. It was understandable. He'd experienced that same sense of injustice and frustration when he'd been shut out of Renata's treatment. It was impossible not to get emotional, even knowing that made you more of a hindrance in the treatment of a loved one.

'I'm sure she's going to be all right. I just wanted to keep you informed.' Certain parts of his anatomy might've been in danger if he'd kept anything from her and something serious had happened.

The lift arrived with a 'ding,' signalling a timeout as they stopped to let new passengers in. They travelled the remaining floors in silence, though he could feel Sophie's rage emanating from the other side of the lift.

He let Sophie lead the way back to the clinic, although it was down to him to get them on the other side of the locked doors and into the treatment room.

'She's in here, resting.' He wanted her to know this wasn't the time for finger pointing. It wasn't going to do Mrs Fields any good to be caught in the midst of their feud.

'Oh, Edith. Are you feeling okay? I'm a terrible friend for leaving you.' Sophie's guilty plea when she saw her frail companion struck Luciano square in the chest. She was blaming herself, even though it had been his decision to send her away.

'I'll survive. Besides, if the doctor hadn't chucked you out I would've done it myself. There's no point in both of us being cooped up in here.' She was pale and weak but Edith hadn't lost her sense of humour. It went some way to easing the tension in the room and Luciano was grateful for it.

He stepped up to the bedside. 'Obviously we want to take every precaution where Mrs Fields is concerned. In case her condition worsens, or she requires long-term treatment, I'd prefer we put her ashore in the nearest hospital. I'm going to need you to pack your bags and disembark at the next port. Unfortunately, Mrs Fields won't be able to continue this trip.'

Luciano had already discussed it with his patient, the news coming as nothing of a shock under the circumstances. She'd even gone as far as joking that this was the reason she'd taken out such extensive travel insurance—a necessity for someone of her age with such numerous health conditions. The medical bills at sea could be enough to bankrupt any unfortunate individual who hadn't had the foresight to take out health coverage. He didn't think it was going to be as easy a conversation with her companion.

Sophie rounded on him, hands on hips, those flecks around her irises blazing like green fire in her otherwise blue eyes. 'You're actually throwing us off the ship now? You really get off on this power trip of yours, don't you?'

Luciano was agog at the vitriol launched at him. 'It's standard protocol. Not a personal decision or a display of any megalomania. We're not equipped to have passengers receive long-term treatment on the ship.'

Sophie didn't back down, maintaining eye contact and managing to sneer at him simultaneously. 'Obviously I'm going to accompany Edith to the hospital but I'd appreciate a second opinion on whether or not she's able to continue her trip.'

'You're well within your rights to do so but it will mean waiting until another doctor is available.' Strictly speaking, the buck stopped with him. He made the medical decisions and reported them back to the captain. It wasn't going to help relations if he confirmed her idea that he was running a dictatorship here.

'That won't be necessary.'

Sophie stood down once Edith spoke, all that spine-strengthening indignation seeping away until she physically wilted into the chair by Edith's bed. 'Whatever you want. We need to get you back on your feet, Edie. That's the most important thing.'

She clasped the woman's hand between both of hers, abandoning the battle with Luciano to focus on her friend.

'Oh, don't worry. I'll have a few days' rest and I'm sure I'll be as right as rain. There's no need for second opinions or to ruin your holiday.'

'But, Edith—'

It appeared Sophie had met her match in this woman, who raised her hand and cut her off in mid-protest.

Perhaps he should ask Edith later for tips on how best to manage riled passengers.

'"But, Edith" nothing. You need this trip more than I do. Why did you think I asked you to come?'

'To—to take care of you?' Sophie stuttered, no longer sounding so sure of herself.

Edith shook her head. 'For you. You've been so despondent lately and I know you hate that job in the care home. The only time I see you come to life is when you talk about the travels you used to have when you were younger. Or when you and Dr Montavano start bickering over me.'

'I do not!'

As she teased Sophie, the mischievous Edith displayed the fighting spirit Luciano was sure wouldn't let her down in her fight back to full health.

He supressed the urge to smile. Any sign of smugness on his part would undoubtedly come under fire from the subject of Edith's well-meaning affection.

'Nonsense. That Ryan clipped your wings and you are someone who needs to fly, or in this case *sail*. You are staying here.'

Sophie scoffed at the suggestion. 'There's no way I'm abandoning you in a foreign hospital while I lounge around a pool.'

'Why not? You can't do anything for me. Besides, I've spoken to John.'

'Your son? Doesn't he live in Spain?'

'Yes, and he's flying in to be with me. Once I'm up and about again I'm going home with him to spend some time with the lovely grandchildren and great-grand-children I rarely get to see. I'll be going to Seville to recuperate and you're not invited.'

'Edith, it's a very kind offer but I don't want to take advantage of your generosity.'

'Not at all. The cruise is all paid for. One of us may as well get the benefit of it and I think a few days away will do you the world of good. Although I will need you to pack my things for me.'

Sophie looked at him as though expecting him to back her up. This definitely wasn't his jurisdiction. 'It sounds as though Mrs Fields has it all planned out.'

'It certainly does.'

Not only did it mean Edith would be in the best place for after-care but Sophie would have no reason to venture into his domain and upset the status quo. He wasn't going to argue and he wouldn't advise Sophie to either.

'Can I at least accompany her when she's transferred to the hospital to make sure she's settled in?' She deferred to him, her whole demeanour changing as she asked him for the favour.

'If you'd like. The ship won't be sailing until later tonight. I'll let the captain know what's happening. I'll be travelling to the hospital too to oversee the transfer of Edith's care.' If anything was going to put her off the idea, he was sure it would be the thought of spending more time with him.

'As the attending physician I'd expect nothing less.' She batted her eyelashes. No doubt an attempt to lull him into a false sense of security before she launched another verbal attack on him.

'Chief Physician,' he added, in the hope his status would give him more authority in her eyes. All he received in response was a raised eyebrow.

As long as they made it back on board before the ship set sail and they weren't stranded together for the night, he supposed they'd survive. At least they'd have Edith and the paramedics as a barrier between them until then.

It was odd that two people who barely knew each other should immediately clash the way they had. Especially when, or perhaps it was because, they worked in the same field. Usually the nurses deferred to him in matters of treatment and, likewise, he respected their position and input. For some reason there was friction, a spark between them where there ought not to be one. Whatever was causing that flash of passionate temper, he hoped to avoid it in the future.

With any luck, once Edith was settled and they were back on board, they'd go their separate ways. Sophie clearly needed the holiday her friend wanted for her, chilling out by the pool. Leaving him free to return to the sanctity of his clinic, where they needn't run into each other again for the duration of her vacation.

His place of work on board was supposed to help him escape thoughts of his late wife and the idea everyone had that he should find someone new.

So how had one woman managed to barge her way in and upend those plans?

CHAPTER THREE

KICKING BACK AND emptying your head of all thoughts except your own enjoyment wasn't as easy as Sophie remembered. She and Dr Montavano had waited until Edith had a bed at the hospital and they were up to date with her medical notes before leaving her. They'd travelled back to the ship in a taxi together, making polite small talk whilst avoiding another clash.

That should've ended all contact between them. Unfortunately, as she was unable to get a phone signal out on the high seas, she had to rely on updates from the good doctor to catch up on Edith's condition.

'Are you back again?' It was Patrice, the nurse who'd first attended to Edith, who spotted her in Reception.

'I wondered if you'd heard anything from the hospital today about my friend, Edith Fields?' She walked over to the desk, bypassing the receptionist to speak directly to the nurse, cutting out the anticipated conversation about how everyone was too busy to speak to her.

Sophie had since apologised to her fellow nursing colleague for her behaviour, which Patrice had graciously accepted, meaning there was only one other person left onboard for her to be awkward around.

'Dr Montavano was in contact with them earlier. Let me go and get him and he can tell you himself.'

'That's really not necessary. I don't want to disturb him.' Sophie's plea fell into the void left by Patrice's departure.

She let out a sigh, resigned to the fact that she'd be forced to see the doctor again. It was difficult enough to get him out of her head without seeing him first thing in the morning. She didn't need a refresher of how good he looked in his whites.

Okay, she sounded as shallow as all those other women swooning over him as he passed by. Deep down, she knew it was more than the physical attraction she was trying to swerve. There was something between them masquerading as a personality clash that was threatening to get in the way of her own self-discovery.

As well as serving as a companion to Edith, she'd hoped this trip would help her rediscover the woman she'd once been. Once upon a time if a guy had taken her fancy she wouldn't have thought twice about acting on that impulse. She hadn't worried about the consequences of asking a man out or what their future held. Back then she'd lived in the moment. These days she was a much more cautious character. Her time with Ryan had made her think more carefully about getting involved with anyone. Especially when the person who'd caught her eye couldn't seem to get rid of her fast enough.

'Ms Blythe?'

There was that whoosh of blood in her veins again at the sound of his silky Italian voice. Until now she'd associated it with their disagreement over Edith's treatment. Watching him striding towards her, she wondered if the increase in her blood pressure was for an entirely different reason.

The dark hair, tanned skin and that dreamy doctor façade had the same effect on most people. It was possible her attraction towards him, unwanted and ill-timed though it was, had manifested in an outburst of temper instead.

She realised she'd been staring at him

wordlessly since he'd said her name. 'I, er, just wanted to find out if there'd been an update on Edith's condition. I didn't mean to disturb you.'

'It's fine.' He smiled, doing his best to put her at ease instead of making her feel she was wasting his time.

Her stomach flipflopped in the same manner as those pancakes she'd watched the chef tossing at breakfast.

'She's comfortable and had a good night's sleep. I hope you did too.'

She cocked an eyebrow at that. That sounded more personal than their usual conversation about their mutual pensioner patient.

'I mean, I hope you weren't up all night worrying.' He went to lean a hand on the edge of the desk but missed, almost resulting in a comedy prat fall. For a moment she wondered if he'd become equally as flustered around her as she had around him. Then he straightened up, looking as smooth and in control as ever, making her believe she had imagined the whole thing.

'I managed a few hours' sleep. Thank you.'

'Good. Well, I should...' He pointed down

the corridor, indicating his need to get back to work.

'Yes. Sorry. If it's easier for you I'll ask at Reception for updates from now on.'

'It's not a problem at all. *Ciao*.' He was walking backwards down the hallway, giving her one last smile before turning away.

Sophie watched until his tight white trousers disappeared around the corner out of sight before letting out a long breath. She wouldn't admit to it being a sigh. The whole exchange had been odd. A completely different atmosphere from the one when they were around Edith. An awkward dance between two people afraid of what might be happening despite outward appearances. She wasn't sure what to make of it but one thing was certain, it was the most excitement she'd had in a very long time.

Sophie chose one of the blue plastic loungers around the main pool. Not so close she'd get splashed every time someone dived in but near enough to jump in herself without having to parade around in her bikini if she decided on a swim. She wasn't used to all this spare time and unless she wanted to join the class making origami animals out of towels on the mezzanine deck, this was the best place to be.

There were the party people here for drinks, music and a good time, children chasing each other round the pool and helping themselves to cookies and ice cream from the all-day buffet. Then there were the people like her, here to soak it all in. She laid her towel down and settled back with her holiday read, making the most of the opportunity Edith had given her for a rest.

Although she was scanning the words and turning the pages of her book, she wasn't really taking it in. It wasn't the sound of children shrieking or the loud music disturbing her enjoyment, it was the noise going on in her own head. There was too much to think about to let her concentrate. Apart from her worry about Edith's health and the crush she'd apparently developed on the ship's doctor, she was thinking about the changes she wanted to make back home. Moving away, changing her job were things she used to do all the time but she was afraid of making the wrong decision. Again.

Ryan's betrayal made her question her own judgement, the choices she'd made and the person she'd become. She'd spent so long as part of a couple she'd lost an important part of herself: her independence. Never would she leave herself so vulnerable again by letting someone dominate her life.

She was about to give up all pretence of reading when a flash of something in the pool caught her eye. Putting her book down, she stood up to get a closer look. There it was again, a splash in the furthest corner of the pool. The deep end was empty with everyone else messing around in the shallows with inflatables, more concerned with showing off than actually swimming. Even the lifeguard was posing for selfies.

She peered down over the edge of the pool and saw a dark shadow shimmering underwater. That was when it hit her. The small splashes and flash of colour had been someone in trouble. Their last gasp for air before they'd sunk to the bottom of the pool.

Sophie didn't think twice about diving in. She held her breath, swimming down and down until she reached the dark mass. With her hands hooked under the arms of whoever was down there, she hauled the dead weight back to the surface with her, gasping for air with the effort. It was a child, not more than seven or eight, but she didn't have the energy left to get him out of the pool, her lungs burning as she fought for breath.

'It's about time,' she snapped at the lifeguard who suddenly appeared, helping to haul the boy out.

'I didn't see—'

'No, you didn't.' She was furious he hadn't been doing his job properly but his negligence wasn't uppermost in her mind.

'He's not breathing.'

The now fully alert lifeguard felt for the child's pulse while Sophie got herself out of the pool. She was sure he had to have first-aid training to get this job but right now she wasn't convinced about any of his credentials so she checked the boy herself. No pulse. His chest wasn't moving, there was no sound of breathing, and he was unresponsive to her attempts to rouse him.

'Go and get help,' she shouted to anyone listening.

They'd attracted something of a crowd as people gathered around, watching the drama of a life-or-death situation as though it was part of the onboard entertainment. If they hadn't the decency to help or turn away, that was down to their own consciences. She couldn't be distracted from saving this child. There was bound to be a defibrillator somewhere on board, as well as the medi-

cal staff. Until either became available it was
down to her to get this boy breathing again.

She brushed her wet hair away from her
face before tilting his head back. With no
visible obstructions to his airways, she
pinched his nose closed and started CPR.
Forming a seal over his open mouth with
hers, she blew until she saw his chest rising. It fell as she took her mouth away and
she repeated the process another four times.

'Joshua? Let me see him. That's my son.'
There was a kerfuffle somewhere to the
side but Sophie let the lifeguard handle the
fraught parent as she started chest compressions. With her fingers interlocked, the heel
of her hand placed in the middle of his chest,
she pressed down hard. She kept her arms
locked out straight, pushing up and down,
doing her best to keep his heart pumping.

'Come on.' She urged him to pull through,
blocking out everyone and everything else
around them.

Working with elderly patients she should
have been used to dealing with death but it
didn't make it any easier. This was a child,
someone who had his whole life in front of
him. He was on holiday, for goodness' sake.
She wasn't going to let him die.

After several rounds of rescue breaths and

chest compressions, she felt movement. He spluttered, coughing up the water lodged in his lungs, his lips slowly losing that deathly blue tinge. Before she breathed her own sigh of relief, she quickly moved him into the recovery position, rolling him onto his side to keep his airway clear.

'Excuse me.' The crowd parted as Luciano appeared with his medical bag. He paid no attention to the water pooled all around as he knelt down beside her.

'He was non-responsive when I pulled him from the bottom of the deep end but I kept on with the rescue breaths and chest compressions until he came around. He's coughed up a lot of water but I think he's okay.'

'Good job, Sophie. I'm glad *you* were paying attention.' Luciano shot the lifeguard a filthy look that would have him fearing for his job, and rightly so. With so many passengers, many of them children, someone in his position had to be vigilant at all times.

'I only saw him because it happened right in front of me. Anyone would've done the same.'

'Are his parents here?' Luciano stood up and addressed those standing around. Once the boy's mother and father made themselves known, he dismissed everyone else with that air of authority that came so easily to him. 'We'll get him down to the medical centre and check him over. What's his name?'

'Joshua.'

'Okay, Joshua, we're going to move you, but Mum and Dad are going to come with you.'

Sophie pulled a towel from the nearest sunbed and covered their little patient until they could get him to the medical centre.

'You too,' Luciano said, grabbing another towel to drape it around her shoulders. It was only then she realised she was shaking, her teeth chattering as the shock of what she'd just done set in. He bundled up her clothes into his arms before they left the scene. This time there was no argument as she let him lead her back into the belly of the ship.

'Something for the shock.' Luciano set a glass of coloured liquid on the desk in front of her.

'Thanks.' She cradled the glass in her hands for a while before she took a sip. The strong alcohol burned on its way down her throat but it did manage to warm her up. Since Luciano had taken over the medical treatment, she didn't think she'd stopped shaking.

'Joshua is fine, thanks to your quick actions. I'm sorry if I've been dismissive of your medical expertise up until now. I know how hard you must have worked to save Joshua and all I can do is apologise.'

She could tell he wasn't a man to say such a thing without complete sincerity, and was grateful for his acknowledgement of her abilities.

'It's all right. I know I was a bit of a handful at first, showing up here telling everyone how to do their job.' If he could admit to his failings, so could she. It might help reduce some of that tension that seemed to accompany their interactions.

'I would've done exactly the same in the circumstances. Now, is there anything else I can get for you?' He got up off the desk where he'd been sitting and Sophie realised she was being dismissed. It had been a long afternoon, he had patients to tend to, and she'd taken up enough of his time. He'd lent her his office to get changed into the clothes she'd retrieved from her sun lounger before they'd come down here. The chat and the drink had been his way of making sure she was all right and wasn't actually going into clinical shock. She appreciated the concern, even if she was put out it wasn't more than a professional interest in her welfare he was showing.

'No. I'll let you get back to work.' She tossed back the rest of the brandy, ignoring the fiery trail it was leaving in its wake, and set the empty glass back on his desk. 'Thanks for that.'

'No problem. I'm sure we'll see each other around.' He had the door open now, seeing her out.

'I'm sure we will.' The prospect set her mind conjuring up ways of avoiding him in the future. She was concerned about what another meeting would do to her equilibrium when she couldn't get control of her emotions around him. Worryingly, there was also a part of her looking forward to it.

'Room for one more?' Luciano managed to bounce onto the excursion bus as the driver was about to close the doors.

'There might be a seat left at the back, Doc.'

'Thanks.' He slapped a hand on Giovanni's back. The twenty-something tour guide worked for the travel company that was contracted to the cruise liner. They transported passengers from the ship to the local tourist attractions and brought them back before the ship set sail for the next destination.

He'd crossed paths with Giovanni and a few of his colleagues before, on the occasions the heat and exertion during the tours had taken their toll on some of the holiday-makers.

As the driver started the engine, Luciano made his way down the aisle.

'We don't usually see you out and about, Doctor.' The cheery rep revealed his identity to the others on board the bus who might not have recognised him otherwise. He'd dressed casually today in the hope of blending in so he could remain incognito. Now his cover had been blown he braced himself for the onslaught of conversations based around the ailments of his fellow passengers. So much for his time off.

'I needed some fresh air.' He didn't intend sharing his thought processes about why he needed to get out and clear his head.

'I'm not sure you'll find it here.' Giovanni guffawed as the bus revved and the smell of diesel filled the interior.

In truth, since Sophie had made herself known to him on board, Luciano had begun to find the clinic as claustrophobic as home.

It was laughable: eight months on board a ship and he'd barely ventured out into daylight.

Before he'd broken the news to her about Edith's health the other day, Sophie had looked so carefree lying on the deck, enjoying the sun. Before the ensuing drama around the pool yesterday, he'd envied her that peace he'd yet to find on board. Today he'd decided to try to find his own. Perhaps a walk on solid ground, enjoying the sights like every other tourist, would do him some good.

He staggered down the bus as it jolted to life, passed all the seats occupied by chattering couples anticipating their next great adventure. He spotted one empty aisle seat and swung into it as the bus rounded a corner.

'Missing me already?' The voice of his co-passenger was unmistakable.

'Sophie? What are you doing here?'

'I was minding my own business until you practically landed in my lap. What are you doing here?'

'The same as everyone else. Sightseeing. It's my day off.' He didn't know whether to be pleased or annoyed that he'd found himself sitting next to Sophie. She appeared to be the only other person travelling solo.

'I would've thought you'd have seen everything a million times over by now.'

'Not recently. I thought it was about time I took advantage of everything the cruise life has to offer.' He was beginning to realise that staying locked away below decks wasn't helping him. He was simply avoiding real life. Although he hadn't anticipated seeing the object of his recent distraction again so soon.

'That includes gatecrashing a bus full of tourists, does it? Admit it, you're stalking me. You just wanted another day in my scintillating company.'

'Naturally.' Teasing he could live with. It was preferable to the fiery exchanges they'd had previously and the confused emotions aroused in him as a result.

Sophie moved her bag from between their seats, allowing him some extra room, and set it in her lap. 'I'm flattered but I can't promise any more thrilling ambulance rides or near-death experiences.'

'Good. I'm off duty. I'd like a quiet day for a change.'

Sophie smiled at him. The worried frown had gone from her brow after yesterday's drama and her eyes were back to that calm grey-blue of the ocean.

Mrs Fields would be pleased that they were beginning to get on.

They sat in silence for a while, taking in the view as the speakers played some cheesy Italian music he supposed was intended to provide a local atmosphere.

'You know, I forget how beautiful this country is sometimes. *Bellissima.*' He watched the muted colours of the green rolling hills pass by the window. They reminded him of home. Of his *mamma* and *papà* out there in the Italian countryside. Likely cooking up a feast for whoever happened to stop by the villa today.

For the first time since leaving his old life behind, he experienced a pang of longing to be back in the bosom of his family. Perhaps it was time to stop running and go back and face life without Renata. By all accounts, Sophie had experienced her fair share of heartache too and she'd survived. According to Edith, she was only just getting back to being herself. He needed to do the same instead of hiding away in the shadows, letting life carry on without him.

'Where is home to you?' Sophie's curiosity pierced his self-reflection, reminding him he'd spoken those first thoughts aloud.

'Barolo. It's vineyard country in the Piedmont region in the northwest. Far from the madness of the city. It's quiet, peaceful.'

'Boring?' Sophie laughed.

'Hmm, more insular, I'd say.' His life had been far from dull. It was ironic he should find more peace aboard a busy cruise liner but along with that came a sense of loneliness. He was missing the family he'd once accused of being too suffocating.

'So you ran away to sea?'

'Something like that.' His laugh rang hollow. That was exactly what he'd done. The trouble was he didn't know what to do next. He'd had his timeout and he knew he wasn't going to sail the oceans for the rest of his days.

'Live in the moment. That's what I want to do too.' Sophie was right. He'd spent too long wallowing in the past, worrying about a future without his wife. For once he should try testing that theory for himself and see if it made him any happier, or life any more bearable.

'Where do we start?' It sounded as though Sophie had more experience in this living-in-the-moment stuff, so he was prepared to follow her lead. If she'd let him.

The bus pulled into the side of the road and the passengers began to file off.

Sophie stood up and slung her bag over her shoulder. 'Right here. Let's just see where our feet take us.'

It was a dangerous game but he was thankful he had Sophie to play it with.

CHAPTER FOUR

SOPHIE'S DAY WASN'T exactly going to plan. Instead of joining the throng of passengers going to the larger cities to check out the tourist traps, she'd chosen to visit Civitavecchia, the town closest to where they'd docked.

She hadn't wanted to fight her way through layer upon layer of sightseers in Rome to bag a five-second glance at something that could never live up to the hype. Especially without Edith. She'd traded their coach trip to see the major landmarks for a more laid-back tour, opting for the slower pace of the local town and certainly never expecting the doctor to turn up as her travel companion.

She'd disembarked without a map or any real plan of where she was going or what she was doing for the day. Luciano, as he'd insisted she call him as this was his day off, had fallen into step beside her as they followed the slow-moving herd into the town centre.

'There's something exhilarating about not knowing where you're going.' They weren't living to any schedule, other than being back before the ship set sail again. Exploring. Her first taste of adventure in a very long time.

'It's not as though we are going to get lost. You can probably see the ship from any part of the town.' He was making fun of her excitement at being let loose but he couldn't possibly understand when he'd been travelling the world, taking it all for granted.

'I'm going to pretend I'm living the dream. Like you.'

That stopped his speed-walking in its tracks. Their fellow explorers carried on ahead, gravitating towards the first souvenir shop they came across. She might take something back for Edith but, personally, she'd rather have a trove of fabulous memories than tacky fridge magnets.

Luciano's scoff drew her attention.

'Hmm?' Her eyes left the contents of the shop window to meet the doctor's scowl.

'What makes you think I'm living the dream?'

She couldn't imagine why her casual remark would upset him. If anything, she should be the one to feel hard done by. They were both working in the same field, yet she was languishing away in a care home with residents who had a busier social life than she did while Luciano was sailing around the sunny Med.

'Sun, sea and whatever else you get up to, in or out of working hours. As much as I love my residents in the nursing home, staring at the same beige walls, day in, day out, can't compare to this.' She only had to glance out at the turquoise sea, sun glittering on the gentle waves, to make her point.

'I suppose it looks like that from the outside but the reality isn't quite so glamorous.' The furrowed lines on his brow smoothed out but his smile only managed to lift the corners of his mouth.

She considered the possible downsides to life on the sea for a few moments but she reckoned that dealing with a few sick or inebriated passengers was worth the constant change of scenery. 'Nice try but my heart is point-blank refusing to bleed for you.'

There was no way she was going to let him feel sorry for himself and spoil today, whatever the reason behind it. As far as she could tell, this was the life she'd always wanted and she hadn't heard anything to change her mind. He should be grateful for the advantages of his position. Some people weren't lucky enough to experience the same opportunities or had given them up in pursuit of an altogether different foolish dream.

At least her apparent lack of compassion managed to draw his mouth into a less mournful smile. Whatever his issue was with his job as ship doctor, it couldn't have been too bad for him to dismiss the subject so easily.

'Where shall we go first?' Fortunately, Luciano didn't come across as someone to navel-gaze too long, leaving his past in favour of their immediate future.

Sophie didn't know how or when they'd become a 'we.' She supposed they'd organically gravitated towards one another as the only solo travellers—not that she was complaining. Excluding Edith, she'd been on her own since Ryan had left and she much preferred company.

Although she'd backpacked alone after university and had enjoyed the freedom, her adventures had always been improved by the people she'd met along the way. Friends, lovers, employers had all been part of her story and now were consigned to the past along with the experience—even Ryan. Luciano was simply a character in her latest tale. Someone she'd mention in passing when recounting her time on this cruise. There was absolutely nothing for her to worry about in spending time with him as long as she remembered that.

Meanwhile, Luciano was waiting for an answer.

'You probably know the area better than I do. Any recommendations?'

He gave a sheepish shrug of his shoulders. 'I told you. I don't get out much.'

There was a lot to unpack from that statement. Given today's surprise it was obviously he could leave the ship if he chose to. He wasn't a prisoner. So why didn't he visit the many ports and cities available to him? More importantly, why had he chosen today and why with her? All these questions—and their answers—would move him from the role of secondary character to something more substantial. She wasn't ready for that.

'Then we need to get away from enclosed spaces and head for the great outdoors.' They continued along the covered walkway until they reached the end of the row of shops. Without the shade provided overhead it was akin to stepping into an oven. A brightly lit oven turned up to maximum heat.

She'd forgotten the sky could be that beautiful shade of azure blue. The sight was only interrupted by the occasional burst of fluffy white cloud. For the last couple of years she'd been convinced the world only came in various shades of sludgy grey.

They broke free from the main thoroughfare and ventured out to the parallel walkway free from people or buildings inhibiting the view of blue on blue.

Sophie rested her hands on the low wall that she supposed was to prevent people from tumbling into the harbour below. She closed her eyes and took a deep breath, inhaling the fresh, salty air of the sea and everything she associated with freedom.

'Anyone would think you'd just been let out of prison.' She sensed Luciano's presence beside her before his laughter reached her ears, and she shivered despite the powerful heat.

'You should be kissing the ground in relief or running through the town naked after escaping your recent incarceration.' It was glib perhaps, but it was her defence against the way he was staring at her so intently. She didn't want to get involved in the minutiae of his life any more than she wished him to be privy to hers. Ignoring the awful pun, they shouldn't be anything more than ships that passed in the night. Not if she was expecting to go home and carry on as though this cruise was nothing more than another experience to cross off her list.

Another hearty chuckle. 'Maybe I will.'

His hands moved to his shirt, undoing his top buttons. Sophie's temperature rocketed. She was mesmerised by the action, watching as he revealed more of his tanned skin and the dark hair nestled there.

'I'm not sure this sleepy town is ready for that.' Neither was she. 'Actually, you look quite at home as you are. International playboy in the playground of the rich and famous.'

She stood up and snapped a quick picture with her camera phone.

'You don't have a very high opinion of me.' He folded his arms across his chest, his short sleeves showing off his nicely rounded muscles. On the contrary, her opinion of him was increasing so much by the second that he'd be in danger of getting a big head if he knew.

'With your clothes and colouring against the backdrop of luxurious yachts you could be easily mistaken for a billionaire businessman. I don't think my pale, freckly skin would fool anyone into thinking I was anything other than English working class.'

'May I?' Luciano held out his hand for her phone, probably wanting to check out the evidence himself. She wasn't expecting to have the camera turned back on her.

'Say *formaggio.*'

'*Formaggio!*' she said with a flourish of her hands as he snapped away.

'See?' He turned the screen so she could see the result of his photography skills.

'Yes, thanks.' It made a change from the selfies she used to take, which had never quite done justice to the scenery she was supposed to have been documenting. He'd managed to capture the soul-restoring essence of the moment with one click.

'You misunderstand. I need you to see yourself as I see you. You look just as at home as I do.'

Reluctantly she studied the picture, concentrating on herself rather than the billion-pound property floating in the harbour.

'I look…happy.' It was a stunning revelation. She couldn't remember the last time her smile had reached beyond her face until her whole body was radiating contentment. Free from the shackles she'd attached when she'd hooked up with Ryan, her true spirit was allowed to soar once again.

'*Sì. Bellissima.*' The compliment warmed her skin as much as the overhead sun but she didn't shy away from it. She felt good so it made sense it should translate to her outward appearance. It was simply nice to hear it from someone else. Unless…

'Is this how you woo all your ladies?' She turned her phone off and shoved it back in her pocket.

'All what ladies? I'm simply telling you that you look beautiful.' He appeared genuinely hurt by her insinuation but pre-Ryan she'd been more streetwise. A lot of British tourists were easily seduced by the romance of a foreign holiday and the handsome locals. In his uniform, surrounded by thousands of women escaping their humdrum lives, it had to be a smorgasbord of vulnerable hearts.

'I'm not naive, Luciano. Women must throw themselves at you. I wouldn't blame you for giving in to temptation. Most men would.' She hopped down off the wall and began walking, the conversation making her irrationally angry. Not least because she'd noticed the gold band glinting on his ring finger for the first time. He hadn't done anything to personally offend her but she resented him on behalf of his absent wife and any easily duped women he might have seduced with that accent and flattering charm.

He wasn't following her any more and when she looked back he'd collapsed onto the wall as though she'd cut him open and removed his entire skeleton. 'I'm not most men.'

She wanted to believe that but it was the type of thing a practised lothario would use to fool a woman into bed. Of course, that wasn't an option now she knew he was married.

'How long have you been working on board? Six months? A year? In all that time you've never succumbed to temptation?'

'Eight months and, no, I haven't been involved with anyone. The cruise company doesn't approve of relationships on board.'

'Oh, so it's not because you're married then?' She nodded at the telltale ring, wondering why she was bothered. He wasn't her husband or her responsibility. Neither was she his conscience.

He lifted his left hand and stared at it as though he'd forgotten he was even wearing a wedding ring.

'No.' He closed the subject down, unwilling to give her any more information on his love life and why should he? Why did she want it? It was none of her business.

Perhaps he was one of the good guys who didn't cheat. It made her feel safer with him knowing he wouldn't try it on with her and make her even more confused about her feelings towards him. He was off-limits.

Unfortunately, that disappointed her as much as finding out he had a wife. She didn't want a relationship or more complications in her life but spending time with Luciano was making her realise she did want something more. If only she knew what.

Luciano should have just told her he was a widower but it wasn't something he shared readily with strangers. For those women who did think he was a candidate for a fling, he flashed his wedding ring in the hope of staving off any further romantic notions. It was his security blanket, his force field to deflect attention about how he came to be here. That wasn't going to work with Sophie. But by voluntarily spending the day with her he was still betraying Renata.

He hadn't so much as looked at another woman since he'd lost her. Now here he was, practically walking arm in arm with Sophie thinking only of how beautiful she'd looked by the harbour. How the sun highlighted the hidden strands of copper and gold in her hair.

It was better if he let them both believe he was still married. There was less of a threat of anything else developing, which would destroy his current peace of mind.

Thankfully she didn't push the subject any further. He hadn't divulged the tragic circumstances of Renata's death to anyone since leaving home and, to be honest, he couldn't be sure how his grief would manifest if he did. It would be mortifying if he broke down crying in the street.

They drifted towards the more populated main boulevard in awkward silence. If they carried on in this vein the day wasn't going to be much fun for either of them.

'The church seems to be something of an attraction. Would you like to go and see inside it?' Anything to relieve the tension, and the silence wouldn't seem so out of place in there.

'Can we just walk in?' He could see Sophie's curiosity was piqued about what so many people were finding fascinating beyond the plain stone façade.

'It's a church. Everyone is welcome.' Seeing her hesitation, Luciano stepped inside first.

'Wow.' Sophie stood beside him, gazing up at the vaulted ceiling then around at the kaleidoscopic colours the sun was making through the stained-glass windows, touching everything with rainbows of light.

It was breathtaking but he felt very much at home here. The religious icons and candles were as familiar as the smell of his mother's perfume.

Sophie, on the other hand, looked every inch the tourist awed by all she surveyed and trying to take it all in.

'You don't go to church?'

'Not really. I'm not going to go up in flames, am I?' Her attempt at a joke at least broke the frosty ground between them again, letting them move on from their previous difficult conversation.

'I hope not. I don't have a first-aid kit or a fire extinguisher with me.'

'Ha, ha.' Sophie gave him an eye roll and took a seat on one of the wooden pews, shuffling along to make room for him too. 'I suppose you're a good Catholic boy?'

'Not recently. I mean, I haven't gone to church as much as my devoted *mamma* would expect.' He hadn't been at all since the funeral. Sailing the Mediterranean was a good excuse, if he disregarded the fact that there was a Sunday service every week. Church was a place for contemplation as well as worship and he didn't need any more time for self-reflection. As it was, sitting here, he was already considering the conversation he'd have to have in the confessional.

Forgive me, Father, for I have sinned... it's been two years since my last confession. Since then I've taken the Lord's name in vain, abandoned my family and my faith, and been unfaithful to my late wife in my thoughts.

'Penny for them...or is it a euro here?'

Sophie broke through his imaginary soul-cleansing. 'Sorry?'

'You're lost in thought. Is everything okay?'

'*Sì. Grazie.* I'm thinking about home.'

'Would you prefer if I gave you some privacy?'

This was an opportunity for them to part ways and put an end to whatever was going on between them. If he stayed here he knew he'd end up walking into that confessional and unburdening his soul. The trouble was, he was afraid he'd hear those words he'd been running away from. That there was nothing wrong with wanting to move on from his grief.

'That's not necessary. Actually, I fancy a drink. Why don't we make our way to the town square and find somewhere to sit in the shade?' He was enjoying the cool interior of the church compared to the heat outside, even if being here beside her was beginning to make him sweat.

'You don't have to ask me twice. I've never drunk so much in my life, trying to stay hydrated.'

Before they left, he made sure to light a candle for Renata, and the babies who had never lived to grow up, silently begging for her forgiveness for any actions that could be construed as inappropriate.

Sophie hovered nearby, giving him the space he needed, though she could have no idea of the turmoil going on his head. She asked nothing from him and backed off when she sensed he needed it, something no one else in his life had managed to do so far.

There was a slight incline up towards the main square. Far enough in the heat that by the time they reached the first al fresco café in the *piazza*, Sophie was ready to collapse.

'Will this table do?' Luciano pulled out a

chair for her under the shade of a free-standing canvas parasol.

'Anywhere will do. I need *acqua*.' Then she spotted the cocktail menu propped up in the middle of the table. 'Ooh!'

'What would you like to drink?' Luciano must've been feeling the increase in temperature too as he loosened another button and exposed more of his manly chest.

'Hmm, something blue.'

That made him laugh. 'That's the only requirement you're looking for in a drink?'

'Yeah. Why not? Let's live dangerously. What about you? What's your drink of choice?'

'I don't mind the odd glass of red wine with my dinner. Otherwise I don't drink in case I get called out.'

'You're not on duty. Someone else is covering today, aren't they?'

'Yes, but—'

'Technically you're on your holiday today too. Besides, I'd look like a lush sitting here drinking on my own.' She didn't really mind. Everyone else here was sitting back and chilling with their assorted alcoholic beverages, too deep in conversation with one another to care what she was doing. It wouldn't do Luciano any harm to relax too.

Especially after their tense exchange over his relationship status. She didn't want him to think she cared.

'I'll have the green one,' he said, closing the menu.

'Good man.' It wouldn't be long before the whole cheating accusation she'd thrown at him would soon be forgotten.

He ordered their drinks from the harried waitress who appeared at their table and seemed relieved to have someone to converse with in her native language.

Sophie managed a feeble *'Grazie...'* and wished she'd learned a few phrases before travelling.

Italian was such a sexy-sounding language. Although, by the way the doe-eyed waitress was fawning over Luciano it wasn't only the language causing a ripple in the female staff.

Their drinks arrived with a dish of roasted nuts to snack on. They sipped at their colourful cocktails, trying not to let the decorative umbrellas and paper parrots perched on the glasses get stuck up their noses. Across the square a young woman set up a microphone stand and amplifier in a shop doorway. Soon they were being serenaded by the haunting out a chaperon. Surely one would eventually wonder what he was getting up to for the best part of a year?

Luciano gave a heavy sigh before he tossed back the rest of his drink. It seemed for ever before he finally spoke. 'My wife, Renata, died two years ago.'

'Oh.'

'Oh.' The pain he must've suffered and which she'd likely made him relive struck her with force in the chest.

'I'm so sorry. I had no idea or I would never have brought the subject up.' She'd more than put her foot in it, she'd kicked him right in the gut because of her suspicious mind.

'You didn't know. I don't talk about it. I should. That's what they tell you to do, right? Talk it out, express your feelings instead of bottling everything up. It's easier for the heart to go along with people's assumptions than put them straight.'

'I can understand that.' Every time she spoke about her relationship with Ryan it ripped open a wound, although in Luciano's case it was over the loss of his wife, not because he felt sorry for himself.

He had been married. She'd died. Sophie couldn't begin to fathom that kind of loss.

sounds of opera, making it a perfect moment that Sophie wanted to remember for ever.

'This is the life I should've had.' She leaned back in her chair, sipping her bright blue drink, soaking up the atmosphere.

'What's stopping you from having it now?'

When she looked at Luciano rocking back on two legs of his chair she wondered that herself. It had been a while since Ryan had left so the only person stopping her from doing what she wanted now was her.

'Responsibilities, bills, financial stability. All of that boring adult stuff.'

He set his chair back onto solid ground and put his drink on the table. 'Correct me if I'm wrong, but that doesn't sound like you at all.'

'I'm not sure if I should be offended by that.'

'Not at all. You seem strong-willed and I can't picture you not following your heart, that's all.'

Sophie tutted. 'That's what caused all the trouble in the first place.'

One glance at his puzzled face and she knew she had to explain. She was sure Edith had blabbed about her troubled love life since, given half the chance, she had been trying to matchmake Sophie with every attractive man she met.

'I was happy living wherever I laid my sun hat. Until I met Ryan, fell head over heels and followed him back to England. I was convinced he was the one I was going to spend the rest of my life with, raising babies.'

'It didn't turn out that way?'

'Does it ever?'

'I guess not.' He swirled the luminescent liquid in his glass, his mind flitting somewhere else that obviously wasn't happy terrain.

'I got bored and made the mistake of telling him so. That prompted him into running off to Las Vegas to marry his work colleague. He's off living it up in America somewhere and I'm left with a mortgage and a job I'm only doing to pay the bills.'

'That must've hurt…but it means he wasn't the one for you.'

'I'm not convinced there is a "one" any more and only a fool would believe that a single person in this whole universe is able to make your life complete.'

'You've had a bad experience, that's all. If you're so unhappy with what you're doing,

why don't you quit? Take that leap and something that excites you?'

'Once upon a time I wouldn't have thoug twice about doing that and I never imagine I'd say this, but I'm scared it wouldn't wor out. Not all of us are guaranteed to land the job of our dreams.' Call it experience or maturity but she no longer had that throw-caution-to-the-wind attitude she'd once lived by. Not when the consequences could strip away your very being.

'What's the worst that could happen?'

'Um, I could end up broke and homeless.' She had no ties but neither did she have any support around her if she lost everything on a whim.

'Well, it's definitely the best decision I've made recently.' He tossed a handful of nuts into his mouth before raising his glass in a toast to his seemingly perfect life, but there was something about the gesture that didn't sit comfortably. As though he was as miserable as she was deep down.

'How is your wife okay with you working away so far and so long from home?' She knew people had all sorts of modern marriages these days and sometimes you had to go where the money was, but it would take a great deal of trust to let Luciano loose with-

Everyone who'd left her had done so voluntarily and, though difficult, she'd come to accept it. To have someone you'd loved enough to marry, expected to spend the rest of your life with, only for them to be taken away must've been devastating. It was no wonder he'd been so defensive, so reluctant to open up. Yet she'd forced this out of him to satisfy her own curiosity and need to know more about him. Now she was responsible for ripping that painful wound open again with no way of closing it.

'We were only married for three years. Together for four but a short, tragic marriage nevertheless. We lost two babies during that time.'

Ugh. This was painful to watch as he stared into the depths of his empty glass. Even the parrot was wilting with the heavy weight of the conversation.

'That's awful. I'm so sorry.' She didn't know what else to say without it being a cliché.

She was so young.
I didn't know her but I feel your loss.
There are plenty more fish in the sea.

That last one was the worst. Something trotted out after every break-up, but it certainly wasn't appropriate in these circumstances. In Luciano's case there probably weren't any more fish in the sea. Not one he wanted anyway. That explained how he'd avoided any romantic entanglement so far. His heart had been broken beyond all repair. Then there were the babies. This was a man who'd had hope of a family, only to have it cruelly snatched away from him. And he'd been left on his own. It was too much to comprehend.

'Not your fault. After her second miscarriage she developed sepsis. No one realised, not even me, until it was too late.' As a medical professional, Sophie knew it wouldn't have been as easy as that to accept her fate. Luciano was a good doctor and as such would've beaten himself up over not spotting or treating the problem himself in time to save her. The guilt was there in the slump of his broad shoulders, much as he might deny it.

'The cruise life was a new start for you?' She had wondered why a well-established doctor would abandon everything he knew and had worked for to live such a transient life. His position would've suited someone with no family or ties to any one place. Someone like her before she'd made the mistake of falling in love. Love ruined your life when it didn't last for ever, like they told you it would in all the fairy tales.

'I'm not sure it was about making a new start. More like avoiding one.' He winced at the admission but she appreciated the honesty. Perhaps that was what she'd been doing in her twenties. She hadn't simply been a free spirit, just a lonely child afraid to return home where there was no one waiting for her.

'How so?' Sophie picked at the corner of a cardboard coaster lying on the table, slightly soggy from the condensation dripping from her glass. She didn't want to appear eager to know all the gory details of what had brought Luciano to this point in his career, even if it was true.

'I know they mean well but my family is pushing me to find someone else.'

'You're clearly not ready for that.' Her acknowledgement opened a chasm deep in her chest, which she chose to interpret as empathy for his loss.

It took him longer to respond to that than she expected. 'I didn't want to think about life without Renata but my family were making it impossible. We're such an Italian stereotype. Lots of siblings, always a new baby to celebrate with vast amounts of pasta and wine.'

'Sounds heavenly to me.' Especially to a woman who'd been way too long on her own and whose idea of a home-cooked meal was something reheated in a plastic container.

'I suppose it was for a while but it's difficult when you need time to yourself and space to breathe.'

'I wouldn't know. Can't say I ever knew my father well. He was a musician. A wandering spirit, apparently. My mother, well, she goes wherever her heart takes her. One wrong 'un after another. I don't see my parents enough for them to suffocate me.' It was incomparable to whatever Luciano had been dealing with but it was her truth. She wanted to find some way of relating to him so he wouldn't regret sharing any of this with her. If he'd run away to sea after losing his wife, chances were he needed someone to talk to. She wasn't a counsellor by any means but everyone needed to vent. Poor Edith had been the closest thing she'd had to a sounding board and look where she'd ended up.

'Swap? I'm sure my *mamma* and *papà* would love to shower you with affection and food.'

'Mine would happily ignore you and give

you all the space you want.' Sad but true. 'Be honest now, aren't you missing your family a little bit?'

It was only when Ryan had gone and she'd been on her own in their house that she'd realised how alone she was in the world. Little wonder that Edith had felt sorry for her to the point of booking her onto a cruise.

She really had to get herself out there and get a life again. This trip, today with Luciano, was the most she'd socialised in months. It was beginning to look as though the same was true for him. Perhaps this was the nudge they both needed to make some changes.

'Hmm…' He contemplated her question for so long she could almost visualise the list of pros and cons he was drawing up about his family in his head. 'A little homesick but I'm not ready to return.'

Sophie's heart gave a hop, skip and a jump. Goodness knew why when she was the one going home in a few days' time. They weren't about to sail off into the sunset together. The best she could hope for was to live her travelling dream vicariously through him.

'I know the feeling. I mean, without the homesick part. If I never went back it would be too soon.' It wasn't so much the place, or even the weather. No, it was the memories. Such dreams she'd had when they'd settled down. Now England represented the end of them. The idea of going back to an empty home and the daily grind of her job filled her with even more dread now she'd experienced something infinitely more thrilling.

'Everybody thinks that when they're on holiday. Perhaps you could extend yours for a week or two?' Was it her imagination or was there a hint of hope in his suggestion? Wishful thinking on her part or not, it wasn't an option.

'Even if I could get the time off work I couldn't afford it. I'm here due to the kindness of Edith's heart, bless her.' The only reason she could enjoy herself now was the knowledge that her friend was recuperating at her son's home in Spain and being spoiled as much as she deserved.

'I know you're a nurse but you didn't say where you worked.'

'In a care home for the elderly. Don't get me wrong, I love them all but I don't think I was made to stay in one place too long.'

'You should see if there are any vacancies with the cruise company in that case.' He grinned, as though daring her to prove she had the guts to actually make the same life-changing decision he had. It made her want to call his bluff, prove to him, and Ryan—and more importantly to herself—that she wasn't simply all talk.

'Maybe I will. I'm willing to sign on as a cleaner, dishwasher or barmaid at this stage.'

'Don't sell yourself short. We'd be lucky to have someone like you in the medical bay.' From anyone else it would've sounded nothing more than professional courtesy. It was the look in his eyes as he held her gaze across the table that made it more personal.

The sincerity of his comment was heightened by the fact that the opera singer had taken a break and his was the only voice to be heard in the sudden hush. The second Luciano realised it his cheeks flushed the same colour Sophie imagined hers were.

'Oh, I don't know. We seemed to clash a little bit when we met. It's probably not conducive to a good working relationship.'

'It shows we're both passionate. I mean, about our work and patients.' Before Sophie had a chance to consider what other ways they could get passionate together he scraped his chair back along the ground and was on his feet.

'I should go and get the bill.' He disappeared into the shadowy recess of the café where she couldn't see him or scrutinise his expression.

For someone who'd gone to the lengths of leaving his family rather than entertain the idea of getting involved with anyone else, he was becoming increasingly flustered at the idea of them spending more time together.

Luciano wanted to get back to the ship and the sanctity of his medical centre as soon as he could. It hadn't occurred to him that disembarking at the nearest port would take him so far out of his comfort zone.

'Let me pay half.' Sophie pulled out her purse when he returned to the table.

'Not necessary. You have the all-inclusive drinks package. Remember?' The joke as they left was supposed to diffuse some of the tension and confusion he'd created with his effusive praise. Instead, as he caught her appreciative smile, his emotions were jumbled all over again.

She was everything he was supposed to be getting away from in this vagabond life. Yet he couldn't stay away and didn't want to. They could have gone their separate ways at any time—when they'd got off the coach, or after their argument at the harbour—but he continued to push his personal boundary, waiting and wondering what their next moments together would bring.

He never imagined he'd open up about Renata, but Sophie was a compassionate person. Enough that he could trust her not to create any drama or tears over his secrets. Just simple understanding.

There was the possibility he'd told her in the hope of creating more distance between them. A widower came with more emotional baggage than the average person. Plus, bringing Renata into existence here should've blocked those developing feelings he was having towards Sophie with guilt.

He didn't understand what was in her genetic make-up that made her so different from all the other women he'd encountered or how she'd made him see that the comments from his family, which had once angered him, came from a place of love.

He didn't have to settle down any time soon. They'd simply wanted him to move on from mourning and at least date again. To think about someone other than his dead wife. He was certainly doing that now but it wasn't bringing him any more peace. Sophie would be leaving soon, on her way back home and out of his life for good. If he ventured back into the world of dating or seeing anyone as more than a friend or colleague, it should be with a free spirit such as Sophie. At least then he wouldn't be torn in two by the idea of permanently replacing Renata in his heart.

Sophie had made it clear that life as a couple wasn't for her—along with staying in one place for too long. He enjoyed her company, was attracted to her, and he was sure after their initial personality clash she felt the same. He simply wasn't sure how far out of his comfort zone he was prepared to go. Perhaps he'd take her advice and see where his feet, his head and his heart took him. Live dangerously for once.

CHAPTER FIVE

'THERE'S A BEACH. Do you think we have time to take a paddle? Just so I can say I've been in the Med?'

'Sure.' The slight detour meant it was going to take them longer to return to the ship but it was impossible to refuse the simple request when her eyes were sparkling like the sea at the prospect.

'It's beautiful down here. I thought it would've been packed out with sun-worshipping tourists.'

It was an impressive panoramic view. The palm trees provided intermittent shade along the broad promenade stretching along the vast extent of the golden sands. Other than themselves, the only souls experiencing the beauty were skateboarders, who were more interested in the smooth lines of concrete available.

'They'll all be fighting for breathing room

at the more popular tourist sights but there's a lot to be said for the less well-known parts of the country. You have time to appreciate everything unspoiled by the tourist market.'

'Like your home town?'

'Yes. We have some of the most beautiful countryside you could ever hope to see.'

'Maybe I will someday.' Sophie's big eyes searched his face for an answer he wasn't willing to give. But promising her a visit, issuing an invitation that suggested a continued acquaintance beyond this week, went against everything he was trying to establish.

'It's off the beaten track.' He knew she would love exploring the vineyards, seeing the colourful wildflowers growing by the side of the country lanes near his parents' home. Funny how he still thought of that as his home. The one he'd shared with Renata, where they'd pictured having a family and growing old together, had been lying empty and unloved since he'd left. Not unlike his heart.

It would be too painful to go back there but going home to see his family might be bearable if he had Sophie there with him. He was relaxed around her, their conversation easy, the mood light. The opposite of everything he'd left behind.

'That's what I was kind of hoping for, but I was angling for an invitation or, you know, directions.' She nudged him playfully with her arm.

'Angling? You want to go fishing? I'm sorry we don't have any rivers near where we live.' If it was a particular hobby she enjoyed he would have to investigate the nearest access. His father would know. It was a long time since Luciano had fished or gone camping as they had done when he was little.

Sophie turned away but not before he saw the grin spreading across her face.

'What? What is it?' He was doing his best to be sincere and honest with himself. Her amusement at his offer struck him like a bullet fired at point-blank range. He was putting himself out there for her. Something he hadn't managed to do for anyone else and she was mocking him? Clearly, he'd read the signs wrong.

'Nothing. Something got lost in translation, that's all. Angling in this case means I was fishing for an invitation.'

'Ah. I see.' The pain gradually decreased. A misunderstanding on his part was much easier to stomach than utter humiliation.

'Sorry. Your English is excellent. My Italian is non-existent. I shouldn't tease.' She reached out and gave his arm a squeeze—an apology, a show of solidarity and the closest he'd come to physical intimacy since Renata's death. Rather than shrink away from Sophie's touch, he welcomed it. It reminded him he was flesh and blood, more than a medical automaton.

There was heat in her touch. Meaning. More than he experienced from merely treating patients. It reminded him he was alive and hadn't died along with Renata. Even if it had felt that way for some time.

He couldn't take his eyes off the slender fingers wrapped around his forearm that provided that connection between them.

The fingers that travelled slowly down his arm to link with his. Hand in hand, Luciano and Sophie stood by the shore as the crystal clear waves lapped gently nearby.

'I've had a lovely day, Luciano.' Sophie's tender voice drew his gaze from their intertwined fingers to her soft lips.

'Me too.' Standing here with her, nothing else existed. It was a memory no one else would ever share. There was only one more thing that would make it perfect. Something he'd thought he'd never want to do again.

Yet the adoration he saw in her eyes, and the slight tilt of her chin, was everything he needed to be sure what he was feeling was right and real.

With a dip of his head he was able to meet her lips with his. He closed his eyes, sighing into the blissful sensation of the kiss—soft and tender, yet filled with so much potential for more. Kissing Sophie was a release from the tension he'd been holding inside for days, trying not to act on his natural instinct to do this. He'd found the peace for which his soul had been searching for so long.

With that, his whole body opened up to the possibility of loving again. She'd awakened the passion inside him he'd thought had died long ago.

He wanted her closer and placed his free hand at her waist, drawing her deeper into the kiss.

Sophie wrapped her arms around his neck, pulling their bodies close enough that her body heat was burning him up. Her mouth was scorching against his. That desire they'd mistaken for battling egos was burning fiercely. The need to immerse himself in her and block out the pain that had tormented him for so long was stronger than the need to breathe.

He slid his hands under the thin fabric of her top, relishing the smooth plane of her skin under his fingertips. It would be easy to lose himself with her and forget who he was and why he'd come here. Sophie flicked her tongue against his and he growled. Too easy.

A slow trickle of cold water splashed over his feet and brought him back to earth. The tide had slowly been making its way in as they'd made out. They'd been carried away by the romance of the setting. This wasn't right. He began to withdraw from Sophie as doubt crept back in. It was a betrayal of his late wife's memory, their relationship and everything he'd ever felt for her.

He saw the confusion on Sophie's face, the daze of passion in her eyes as she stepped back. His feet were well and truly soaked through but it was a small price to pay for the return of some common sense.

'We should get back to the bus in case they leave without us. The ship won't wait, not even for me.' He could barely muster a fake smile to accompany the feeble attempt at levity.

'Luciano?' Heart-breaking bewilderment furrowed her forehead. None of this was her fault. He was the one messed up and in the wrong. The one who continued to sin when he continued to lust after her. He still wanted to reach out to those kiss-swollen lips begging for attention and claim them again.

It was only his thumbs he let trace over her tempting mouth before stroking her cheek, knowing he couldn't go back there. His conscience wouldn't let him, despite every other inch of him begging for mercy.

'Sophie… I just can't.' He pleaded with her for understanding. She knew his background and why this was wrong even if it didn't explain why he'd initiated the kiss or why he was walking away now. He couldn't give his heart to anyone else. Especially someone he knew he was getting too close to and who was walking out of his life again in a matter of days. Sophie had made it clear she was no longer the kind of woman who would stick around and he couldn't risk his heart on anything less.

He daren't look back as he made his way across the beach without her. There was a danger that was all it would take to grab her again and give in to that primal need to possess her. Playing out some erotic movie scene as waves crashed over their feverish bodies writhing on the sand wasn't going to make their lives any easier.

They were both in pain and an entanglement between two people who lived completely different lives wasn't going to heal broken and bruised hearts.

This was for the best, no matter how physically painful it was at this very moment.

Sophie would have kissed everyone on board if she'd thought there was a chance of it lessening the impact one man's lips had had on her.

It wasn't as though she'd asked Luciano to kiss her. At least, not in so many words. It had simply…happened. She didn't regret it but the consequences made her wonder if it was worth the hangover. It wasn't the tender bruising of her lips keeping her awake but the sheer force of desire that had caused it. Goodness knew the last time she'd been kissed like that. If ever. Certainly not by Ryan. He'd been safe and predictable, or so she'd thought. Luciano had been pure, raw passion.

The memory rekindled those little shivers of desire zinging along her spine. She slid the balcony doors open and stepped into the night in bare feet. The man was impossible to get out of her head. Even today, walking around the town of Lavorno on her own, she'd thought of him. The cathedral she'd visited alone had made her think about him. Even strolling along the canals, which had once been a gateway for transporting goods to the local markets, had sparked the memory of that private moment with him on the shore.

They hadn't spoken since that breath-stealing scene. Luciano had sat in brooding silence on the short bus journey back to the ship. He'd also been the first one to alight, without waiting for her. She hadn't seen him since. Unfortunately, out of sight didn't equate with out of mind.

It was obvious why he'd pushed her away and she hadn't forced him into conversation or an explanation. His grief was stronger than her feeling of rejection in the pain stakes. He'd told her he was mourning his late wife, to the extent that he'd left home to work anywhere else. Neither of them was in the right head space for a serious commitment, but she would have settled for short term after sharing *that* kiss.

A holiday romance would have done her confidence and libido the world of good but this wasn't the time to be selfish. Luciano was a man in pain and she couldn't take advantage of that vulnerability. Falling for someone mourning his wife and unborn children was a complication she didn't need. Whatever had passed between them was over after that hot, blistering start.

She should think about making more connections on board to prevent her from obsessing over the one person consuming her thoughts. Now Ryan was nothing more than a distant memory she'd chalked up to experience. A day in Luciano's company was all it had taken to bring her back to the woman she'd once been. Passionate, free and living in the moment.

There was a certain kind of calm to be found, standing out her on the balcony with only the stars piercing the darkness. The rush of the waves against the hull below sped them towards a different destination and the change of scenery she needed.

Somewhere far out at sea an orange pulsating light lit up hidden clouds in the sky. The dull rumble of thunder disrupted the soothing swoosh of the waves followed by a whip of lightning cracking open the world above.

The charge of electricity in the atmosphere couldn't compare to what had flashed between her and Luciano yesterday. Yet as the storm grew closer, Sophie knew there was a change coming in the air.

She shivered and the cold blast of air across her skin made her draw her robe tighter around her body. Watching the drama unfold was exciting and beautiful, something she might never experience again in her lifetime. Up close it would be dangerous and destructive and she couldn't help but compare it to her unfurling feelings towards Luciano. She considered herself fortunate to be on the outside looking in rather than caught in the eye of the storm.

Sophie was woken some time later by the rolling motion of the ship and the phone ringing somewhere near her head. With the curtains closed she had no concept of time or place but a quick glimpse at the clock confirmed she'd slept later than intended.

The shrill ringing continued until she picked up the receiver. As far as she was aware, the lines were inter-cabin only so she had no idea who would be ringing her. Her heart fluttered with hope that it would be Luciano, wanting to meet up.

'Hello?' Her voice was husky from sleep and a desire to see him again.

'Sophie? Is that you?' The line crackled with interference but Sophie could just about make out the voice on the other end of the line.

'Edith? Oh, my goodness. How are you?' She sat up, wide awake now and eager for news.

'I'm fine. Hypertension, apparently, which they've given me medication for. A whole lot of fuss over nothing. The family won't let me lift so much as a finger.'

'Good. That's how it should be. You deserve a rest.' At least someone had managed to get her to take a break and it was nice to know she had family around taking care of her—something Sophie was sadly lacking in her own life. There was no one to whom she could unburden herself, no one to put an arm around her and offer support. Apart from Edith, the only one who'd offered her that had been Luciano.

'A rest? I'll have forgotten how to use my arms and legs by the time I go home.' Edith gave a cackle and it was easy to tell she was content in the arms of her family.

'I'm glad you're doing well. How did you get through on the phone? It must be costing an absolute fortune.' She had no idea how technology worked out here but she did know it was expensive trying to get any sort of contact with the outside world.

'That nice young doctor sorted it out. He called to see how I was and thought you might like to hear for yourself.'

Sophie swallowed the shock at the mention of their mutual acquaintance. 'He was right.'

'Such a lovely man.' Edith's dreamy voice suggested she might be harbouring a crush of her own on the handsome Italian.

'What's the weather like where you are? Things are a tad bumpy out here today.' She changed the subject so she didn't have to talk about the man who'd orchestrated a much-needed catch-up between friends— something he hadn't *had* to do either professionally or out of courtesy. He knew she needed it and had gone above and beyond the call of duty to contact Edith for her. Unless he was doing whatever it took to keep her out of the clinic, on the hunt for news herself...

'Awful. Sun, sun and more sun.' Another laugh.

'Make sure you're wearing sunscreen and drink plenty.'

'Don't worry. I'm safely ensconced in the shade with a gaggle of attentive waiters tending to my every need.'

'Sounds as though you're enjoying yourself.' It was a weird thing to say to someone who'd had a serious health scare but Edith did come across as happy and that was all Sophie wanted for her.

'I am but what about you? Are you taking advantage of everything on board?'

Flickering images of her passionate tryst with Luciano as waves lapped around their feet popped into her head, making her blush. 'Er...yeah. I've gone out on a couple of excursions and sampled some of the local life out here.'

'Where are you today? What exciting adventures lie in store?'

Sophie stretched across the bed to jerk the curtain to one side but they were still out at sea in choppier waters than usual.

'I have no idea. I haven't left the cabin yet.'

'What? That's not the deal we had, missy. Now, you get yourself out there and see what life has waiting for you.'

'Yes, ma'am.' Sophie saluted, even though Edith couldn't see her.

'Please thank that delicious doctor of yours again. Such a lovely man.'

'He's not *my*—'

'Go, get yourself out there and I'll see you when I get home.' The phone clicked as Edith hung up, refusing to hear Sophie's denial.

Sophie continued to cradle the receiver in her hand long after Edith ended the call, the dawning truth leaving her in a trance.

No matter how much she tried to deny it, someone hundreds of miles away could tell Luciano was playing a significant role in her latest adventure. In defiance of all inner protests otherwise, Sophie was missing him… all signs she was heading towards disaster. She'd become too dependent on his company being part of her journey. He was in mourning and she was still carrying wounds from her last relationship. She didn't need to add any new ones.

No, she'd thank him for putting her in touch with Edith and discharge the debt she owed him. After that she'd get back to being her.

CHAPTER SIX

'COME BACK TOMORROW and we'll change the dressing for you. In the meantime, I'll give you some painkillers and antihistamines to ease any pain or itching.'

'Thanks, Doctor.' Luciano's young patient eased himself off the bed and gingerly pulled his football shirt back over his head, grimacing as the fabric slid over his burned shoulders.

'Remember to keep covered up, stay in the shade and keep hydrated.'

'Yes, Doc.' The twenty-something English passenger hung his head as he left the clinic but Luciano knew from experience he was fighting a losing battle.

'They never learn their lesson.' Patrice tutted, hands on hips at the latest in a long line of swimmers who had forgotten to reapply sun cream after being in the pool.

'Despite it being a painful, blistered one.'

It never failed to amaze Luciano how much damage people put their bodies through in the space of a week or two. His latest casualty had done it accidentally but there were plenty who purposely went out with little or no sun protection in the name of a tan.

His thoughts immediately turned to Sophie, who was comfortable enough in her own skin not to worry about such vanity. She didn't need to, beautiful as she was with her porcelain skin dusted with sprinkles of freckles. She was such a contrast against his dark, Mediterranean complexion. He was earthy, hardwearing terracotta against the finest English bone china. Exquisite. Elegant. Too delicate to treat carelessly yet too pretty to hide from view.

He was guilty of attempting to do both. It had been a mistake to kiss her, to lead her on the way he had when it could amount to nothing. Trying to pretend she didn't exist either wasn't working. He was aware of her presence even if he couldn't see her.

That was what had led him to contact Edith through the number she'd left for her son. He'd considered it the next best thing to speaking to Sophie herself. They hadn't spoken since the trip but that didn't mean he hadn't been thinking about her, the taste of her or the sensation of having her in his arms.

The abrupt end of that moment had been entirely down to him and the spectre of betrayal haunting his conscience. None of it was fair on Sophie and he hoped the small act of putting her in contact with her friend would go some way to her forgiving him.

When the rap on his office door sounded he hadn't expected to see the woman herself standing next to Patrice.

'There's someone here to see you,' his favourite staff nurse said with a knowing look as she showed Sophie inside then quickly disappeared out of sight. Was it that obvious something had happened between them? He'd hear whatever Sophie had come to say then put an end to whatever was happening between them. It wasn't going anywhere, therefore he wasn't willing to put his job or reputation at risk for one little kiss. Except if that was all it had been, his pulse wouldn't be so frantic at the mere sight of her again.

'Sophie? I wasn't expecting to see you here. Are you unwell?' He rose from his seat to close the door behind her so gossip wouldn't spread beyond the office walls.

'No, nothing like that.' She had one arm wrapped around the other, defensive and ill lids was worse than if she'd called him out on his behaviour. If she'd slapped him, yelled at him for blowing hot and cold, it would have been punishment he'd be willing to take. Now that she knew as well as he did why this couldn't happen, maybe she'd think twice about coming to see him in future.

Sophie scrabbled to find the door handle. It had been a mistake to come here but she'd wanted to find out for herself if his call to Edith had been his way of putting her off visiting. Now she knew for sure the reason wasn't because he didn't want to see her. Quite the opposite and with good reason. Within a few moments they were back to the place that had caused all the trouble.

'I don't know what's happening, Sophie.' Guilt was there in every confused word he uttered. Since she was the one who'd sought him out, she had to be the one to walk away this time and save them both from further torment.

She steeled herself against the door and hardened her heart as much as she could. 'Chemistry, Luciano. I'm sure you've experienced it before, during and after your marriage, with women other than your wife. As you're also aware, you don't have to act

at ease. It did nothing to alleviate the guilt when not so long ago they'd been able to talk so openly to one another.

'I'm glad.' In more than one way… He was happy she was well and also secretly delighted she'd come to see him. Despite his insistence to the contrary, he'd wanted to see her. This way he could deny it was his doing. Fate had intervened—or perhaps it was Sophie's desire for closure.

'I…er…just wanted to say thank you. For the phone call. With Edith.' The short, clipped explanation for her visit wasn't in keeping with her usual chatty manner. It was difficult to tell if she was being abrupt with him—understandably so—or if she was only here out of courtesy. On the other hand, she could be experiencing the same awkwardness he was.

'She's my patient. I wanted to make sure she was okay and it was only a matter of connecting her to your room afterwards. It wasn't a big deal. There really was no need to come and thank me in person.' He was trying to downplay his part but he could see by the sudden hurt clouding her eyes he'd gone about it the wrong way. It sounded as though he didn't want her here when nothing could be further from the truth.

'Right…well, thank you anyway.' She glanced at the door, clearly regretting having come.

He was going to let her go and end their mutual misery when the ship suddenly lurched, unbalancing Sophie and pushing her towards him. She reached out a hand to steady herself against his chest. Instinctively he took hold of her, anchoring his hands at her waist to steady her, their position a re-enactment of their time in the shallows.

'Are you okay?' There was no disguising the thick sound of desire in his voice. He could almost taste the salt on her lips from that day. What would they taste of today? he wondered. They looked sweet and pink like plump strawberries.

'I'm—I'm fine,' she stammered, staring up at him but not breaking contact.

'The sea is rough today. Usually I forget we're even on a ship.' He was rambling, keeping his mouth busy to stop him doing the only thing he wanted it to do. Kiss her.

'I'll have to get my sea legs or I'll be stumbling into people all day.' Her laugh was as shaky as his breathing.

'It's no problem.' As long as it was his arms she kept falling into he wouldn't mind. There was another jolt, a shudder as the

ship forged through more rough water. The sudden, sharp incline of the motion sent them both stumbling back, still caught up in each other's arms.

Luciano let go of her waist to brace his hands on the back of the door before the force of the waves left her crushed between him and the walls.

'Wow.' Despite his efforts to save her from injury, she sounded winded.

'Are you all right, Sophie?' He scanned her face for signs of distress but all he could see was her waiting for something he was afraid to give.

'No.' To his horror he saw tears pooling in her beseeching eyes and he didn't think it had anything to do with any physical injury she'd sustained.

'What can I do to make things right between us?' He brushed his knuckles down her cheek, knowing he shouldn't be touching her but unable to stop himself. It had never been his intention to hurt her but it was a consequence of letting himself believe he could act on their chemistry.

She closed her eyes and shook her head. 'Nothing.'

The pain in her choked response and the hurt she was trying to hide behind closed on it. It's there between us, there's no point in pretending otherwise, but I don't want to make this into something it's not. We aren't about to embark on some great love affair when I'm only on board for another few days. You're clearly not on the market for a holiday fling, which, if we're being honest, is all I'd be interested in. So let's just go our separate ways.'

With a push against Luciano's chest first, she yanked the handle down and let herself out. She wasn't sure how much of that speech *she* believed but someone had to do something. The situation was becoming intolerable, waiting for Luciano to decide if she was worth risking his conscience on.

Her steps quickened as she made her way back down the corridor. There was a fear she would run into a member of staff and give herself away by bursting into tears. She liked him and he liked her but this was still so damn hard.

A thud sounded back from where she'd just come from but she daren't look back. Instead she nodded goodbye to the receptionist and waited impatiently for her to buzz the door open for her to leave.

She wasn't going to attempt to wait for the lift. It was so claustrophobic on this level and she was wondering if a cruise had been the best holiday idea for her after all.

Taking the steps two at a time, she raced up towards the top deck and the illusion of space. Every now and then she imagined Luciano calling her name. Wishful thinking.

She was out of breath by the time she reached her destination but instead of heading towards refreshments or seating she made for the open deck. A sudden surge sent her wobbling across the lobby into the wall.

'Sophie!'

This time she knew it wasn't her imagination. Luciano was standing at the top of the staircase, calling her name. He was only making this harder for both of them. She cursed herself for bringing out this fresh wave of torture.

She released a sigh of frustration that they were going to keep rehashing this. Before she could engage in another battle of emotions with him, there was a deafening roar followed by the sound of glass shattering all around.

The deck was literally pulled from under her as she was swept off her feet by a tidal wave of water. The shock and cold stole her breath away, leaving her splashing around, swallowing mouthfuls of water as she tried to work out what was happening.

As the ship listed, she was carried along at speed beside pieces of broken furniture and crockery. She was hurtling towards Luciano, who was still clinging to the handrail at the side of the steps.

'Grab hold of me!' he yelled over the roaring noise in her ears. Although he was no more than knee deep in the water, she knew once she hit those steps she'd be battered and bruised and goodness only knew if she'd be able to fight her way back onto her feet. All those terrible disaster movies she'd watched as an impressionable youngster came back to haunt her.

As she contemplated her watery grave, her body floating tragically towards the ceiling, there was a tight band of pressure around her chest. She looked down to see Luciano's arm wrapped around her torso.

'Hold on.' Unable to hear anything now bar the rush of water, she had to lip-read his muffled words, but he'd hooked her under the arms and she grabbed his thick forearm like a lifeline. Together they fought against the current until they managed to get her back on her feet.

Luciano manoeuvred her around until she

was able to cling to the rail as he shielded her with his body.

Sirens began to blare around the ship to let them know too late that they were in danger, along with an announcement for all passengers to return immediately to their cabins and remain there until further notification.

'Wh-what's g-going on?' Her teeth were chattering as she coughed and spluttered, trying to catch her breath again.

'I think we've been hit by a rogue wave. Hopefully that's the worst of it over.'

The violent movement was subsiding and the water level, though sloshing around her middle, wasn't rising any faster.

'Where did that come from?' Still winded, she was draped over the handrail like a soggy ragdoll.

'That's why they call it a rogue wave. Sometimes they happen out of the blue when rough seas are nowhere to be seen. They can be anything up to a hundred feet high. I haven't seen one before but I've heard about them.'

'I thought I was a goner.' Her life had actually flashed before her eyes when she'd thought she was about to be whisked off into the dark depths of the ocean or drowned on the lower decks—not in a montage of cinema-slick highlights, rather those past few wasted years and all the things she should have done.

What if she had died? There was so much she hadn't lived or experienced. Regardless of how minor this event might turn out to be, it had only fuelled her desire to grab onto life with both hands the way she'd done to Luciano's arm.

'You're here. You're here.' Luciano rubbed her back with the same solid reassurance she had come to expect from him. He'd be there whenever she needed him. She'd have done the same for him if circumstances had dictated or if she'd been strong enough to hold him up against the current. She'd have done anything to keep him alive, even if it had meant risking herself.

'I'm wet.' Despite everything, she managed a laugh. Luciano was right. Thanks to him there was no real harm done. She'd hug him if she weren't soaked through.

'Let's get you back to your cabin. You need to get warmed up and change your clothes.' He prised her fingers from around the cold steel bar and curled his hand around hers.

'You need to go and tend to your real patients. Although it might be an idea for you to get changed too. We don't want any old ladies fainting at the sight of your entry into the wet T-shirt competition.' His entire outfit was leaving little to the imagination.

It wasn't her intention to make him feel self-conscious but accepting all his attention seemed selfish. Besides, he was only making her want him more when he was being so protective towards her.

'Will it be safe? We don't know what's happened down there.' She couldn't be sure the clothes in her cabin were any drier than the ones she was wearing. For all she knew, they might be safer up here.

'Look at your feet. The water is only ankle-deep now. It was one wave.'

'Rogue.'

A single goodness-knew-how-high wave that had swamped the ship. She'd simply been standing in the wrong place at the wrong time, had got caught in it. They'd hit a pocket of turbulence at sea, which they'd hopefully now passed through. If there were no further incoming swells, they'd only have to mop up the mess this one had left behind.

'A bit like you,' he said with a grin. 'It struck out of nowhere and caused chaos in the brief time it was on board.'

'Charming.' She wasn't sure the comparison was complimentary but she was intrigued by the thought that he found her troubling. Perhaps his feelings about her weren't entirely dealt with just yet.

'One of nature's fun surprises.' Luciano charmed her back onside with a wink. 'Now, let me escort you back to your cabin.'

He took her arm and helped her wobbly legs make it down the puddled steps.

'I'm sure I wasn't the only one hurt. There was a lot of smashing and crashing going on there.'

'Are you hurt? I could carry you back to your cabin.'

'No! Only my pride was wounded. I can walk on my own, thank you.' Being swept up in his arms as he carried her back to her suite wasn't going to help put an end to her fantasies about him. Especially when she was jealous of the way his wet uniform was clinging to his body.

'If you're sure. I want to be certain you're safe.' He was entirely too chivalrous for his own good.

The ship was no longer lurching and now that the danger seemed to have passed the whole place sparked back to life. The sudden sights and loud sounds were overwhelming as she was trying to get to grips with her own trauma. Horns were blaring, followed by further announcements for passengers to return to their cabins and a call for the crew to muster echoed around the hull.

'At least we don't have to go port side with our life jackets on.' If she took Luciano's word for it, the ship wasn't going to sink to the bottom of the ocean regardless of how it sounded.

'Trust me, if that was the case I'd have you deposited in the first available lifeboat by now,' he muttered.

'Doctor, I think you're needed over here.' A blur of uniform paused long enough to inform Luciano before hurtling away again.

'If you're sure you're okay, I'm going to have to go.' He dropped a light kiss on Sophie's cheek and hurried off to don his Super Doc cape for whoever needed him next, leaving her daydreaming about turning her head to meet his lips for another bone-melting kiss.

CHAPTER SEVEN

THE CREW WERE running around, splashing across the decks with buckets and mops on what seemed like an impossible clean-up operation.

He knew there was another doctor on duty today along with the nurses who could take care of any incoming casualties to the clinic. It was those who couldn't make it there on their own he was concerned about. Both he and Sophie had been lucky to avoid serious injury but not everyone had necessarily been as fortunate.

His skin was clammy and not merely because of the soaking he'd endured but at Sophie's near-miss as she'd almost been carried away by the wave right in front of his eyes. His only thought had been to save her. He hadn't cared if he put himself in jeopardy, and he knew that if she'd gone overboard rather than down the stairwell, he'd have gone after her. Putting his own life on the line wasn't something he'd do for just anyone. If he could have sacrificed himself to save Renata he would have, and the same was true for Sophie. Someone he'd only recently met.

Driven by a need to remind himself that she'd survived intact, he'd kissed her again—only a peck on the cheek but he'd *needed* that physical contact, no matter how brief. He didn't know if any of what had happened would change things between them. She was still going back to England in a matter of days. It already felt like a bereavement of sorts, knowing he might not see her ever again.

Whatever lies his conscience had been telling him that putting her in touch with Edith would somehow remove him from the equation, the opposite was true. He'd known deep down that Sophie would seek him out to thank him, absolving him of the responsibility of seeking her out first.

It was selfish, and he was hurting them both by continuing to deny his feelings towards her. Sophie was the one being honest. They both knew what this was between them and he couldn't run away from it for ever. Probably not even for the few days left of her trip. Every moment he spent in her company brought them closer and closer to temptation.

Luciano was beginning to find life on board stifling. He wasn't any more in control of his life here than he had been back on dry land. The only place he felt confident was at work.

'We need some help over here, Doctor.' He was beckoned over to the restaurant, Sophie following close behind, ignoring his instructions to go back to her cabin, ignoring her own bad experience and current discomfort.

'Where do you think you're going?'

'You need all hands on deck. Pardon the pun.' She gave an apologetic shrug for the ill-timed joke but he couldn't deny any help would be gratefully received in the circumstances.

He frowned, unwilling to put upon her but ultimately aware he had to for the good of any injured people.

'I know you're not going to take no for an answer.' Even if he did reject her offer, he knew he'd be wasting his time.

'Correct.' Any potential argument was over before it began.

As they walked back up across the deck, he couldn't help but be aware of the utter

devastation caused during that short dem-
onstration of Mother Nature's power. The
crew were doing their best to sweep up
broken glass, which was ebbing and flowing at the will of the remaining water. The
smell of alcohol around the outdoor bar was
strong. The bottles had been whipped from
the shelves and dashed to the deck in the
melee. Sun loungers were strewn around,
some broken and some floating in the over-
flowing pool.

At least there didn't appear to have been
anyone swimming at the time of impact,
given the lack of abandoned towels around
the area. A squad of crew were like worker
bees, stacking up damaged furniture at the
side like a soggy bonfire. When they walked
into the restaurant, he could see areas of the
ceiling tiles had been broken or shifted out
of place. It was going to take a great deal
of work to get the ship back the way it had
been but it could have been so much worse.

'I need you and whoever else you can get
to help. Go down to the medical bay and get
wheelchairs for us to transport anyone seriously injured.' He sequestered the assistance
of a porter he recognised and issued his orders, remembering at the last second to add,
'Please. I'll need whatever medical supplies

you have available.' One of the chefs who appeared through the galley double doors was promptly despatched back inside by Luciano. It was the area most likely to have a first-aid kit for emergencies. Kitchens were notorious places for all manner of accidents and injury.

Officially, he wasn't the man in charge. That was the captain. But in this instance he felt equally responsible for the souls on board and therefore justified in organising help for the casualties. After all, the captain would be onto him if he thought he wasn't doing his job well enough by putting passengers' safety first.

Whilst he'd been issuing orders, Sophie had set up a triage system using the tables and chairs usually occupied by hungry diners. Those who'd been caught up in the carnage or been hit by falling debris were marked by scarlet stains on their usually pristine uniforms.

'What's the initial impression of casualties?'

'Mostly abrasions and lacerations. A few possible broken limbs in those knocked off their feet or slammed against the wall with the force but we'll need X-rays to confirm.'

Again, Luciano was reminded how fortunate he and Sophie had been not to have suffered more than a few knocks.

The chef returned with the medical supplies that would be needed to patch up the walking wounded. Sophie flipped open the first-aid kit and set to work cleaning and dressing the most serious injuries.

'If you could point out the possible fractures, I'll have them transported down to the clinic for further assessment.'

She separated the casualties into priority groups so Luciano attended those who were most critically injured.

He assessed the injuries himself, coming to the same conclusions as his colleague. Once the wheelchairs arrived, he delegated transportation to the clinic by the more able-bodied among them.

'Careful not to jolt that leg,' he said, helping a porter to lift a young female attendant into a wheelchair, kicking out the stand so she could keep the limb straight. 'Tell them to X-ray that and I'll be down as soon as I can.'

'What do need me to do?'

'You're supposed to be resting.' Her hair still hung damply around her shoulders. He could tell she was one of those selfless people who never thought of themselves. It didn't matter what adventure she craved, she deserved to have someone to look after her too. She didn't seem to have that loving support from family that he'd found overwhelming but was now beginning to appreciate. If he didn't have a clinic full of patients to treat, he'd be tempted to do it himself.

For a start, he'd dry her hair for her. It would be uncomfortable soaking into her supposedly dry clothes. He'd make sure she was tucked up in bed for some much-needed rest after her ordeal and he'd stay to keep an eye on her.

However, any pampering would have to wait until they'd finished with the emergency cases. That had to take priority over his concern for Sophie.

'What I would like to do is take a further look below decks to see if there's anyone else in need of assistance.'

'Lead the way.' Sophie stood aside to let him pass just as the captain made his presence known. Immediately the rest of the crew stood to attention, ready to receive any further orders.

'Doctor, I'd like a full report on casualties, please.' Usually an affable presence on board, the captain's face was stony, no doubt anticipating the bad news he would have to report back to the company and the coast-guard regarding the incident. It was the sort of freak event that, although no one's fault, would bring negative publicity and a stack of paperwork. If that was the extent of their worries, Luciano would be grateful.

Luciano gave him a briefing of what he'd seen so far. 'I'll know more once I get down to the medical centre.'

'I'm going down there now myself if you have everything in hand here.' The captain was going to have his work cut out for him on all levels and Luciano didn't want to hold him back.

'We have. Sophie, one of our passengers and a qualified nurse, has already triaged casualties here.'

It wasn't a favourable look the captain shot at Sophie. More as though she was an added complication he could do without, but he couldn't deny that they needed her.

He took Luciano aside where Sophie couldn't hear. 'Can we get a temporary work contract sorted out? I don't want us getting sued for medical negligence on top of everything else.'

'Of course. I'll get it sorted with head office as soon as I have some free time.' He was keeping his tone courteous, professional. All the while Luciano's jaw was like a steel trap, ready to snap. They were lucky to have Sophie here in a professional capacity. Not everyone would be stepping up like this during their holiday. Sadly, there weren't enough Sophies in the world. Even if she hadn't been medically qualified, he could see she was the sort of person to volunteer her help in a crisis. Captain Superior wouldn't be reluctant to let her get her hands dirty if she'd grabbed a mop to assist with the general clean-up.

There was an abrupt nod before the captain took his leave, apparently not entirely satisfied by what he'd found.

'What was all that about?' Sophie waited until he strode off before enquiring.

'The neurosis of a man who knows he has serious paperwork to fill out. Speaking of which, he wants you to sign something official if you're going to be working in a professional capacity with us for a while. Everyone needs to cover their backs in the world of liability claims.'

'Understandable. I'll provide references and copies of my qualifications too if you need to check them out. You shouldn't just take my word for it that I'm a nurse.'

'Yet I do.' Although, it was more than that.

He'd seen that caring nature of hers enough to know the empathy and kindness that was clearly in the marrow of her bones. What she was capable of could never be adequately expressed on a mere slip of paper.

'Doc, I don't feel so good.' Pavel, the chef who'd supplied the first-aid kit, was leaning heavily on Luciano's shoulder and clutching his side.

'Here, sit down.' Sophie was on the other side of the hefty cook, escorting him towards a seat before his full weight crushed Luciano.

Once Pavel was seated, Luciano knelt beside him on the wet carpet, checking his pulse, whilst Sophie opened the top button on his chef's whites. His pulse was rapid and Luciano could see sweat forming on the man's skin. Luciano held his hand to his forehead and could feel fever burning through his body.

'I need you to tell me exactly where it hurts.'

'Here,' he gasped, and pointed to his lower right-hand side.

Sophie unbuttoned the rest of his shirt to uncover his torso, letting Luciano get a clearer look at his abdomen.

'Did you fall or get hit by anything during the storm?' Luciano pictured solid steel industrial appliances in the kitchen and the force with which Pavel could have been flung against any of it.

'I was ill before the wave hit. I thought perhaps it was too much drink.' He gave Luciano a sheepish look as though he didn't know the crew sometimes partied too much below decks after hours.

It was unsurprising that they let their hair down when they worked so hard with scant free time. Luciano was the exception to the rule.

'When did the pain start?' Luciano applied pressure to the area Pavel had pointed out, causing him to draw a sharp intake of breath.

'Couple of days ago.'

'Do you have any other pre-existing medical conditions I should know about?'

'No.'

'Why on earth didn't you visit the medical centre?' They were there to treat the crew as well as the passengers. Any sign of illness was important to address, especially in someone who worked in the kitchens. He would've been treated straightaway. With so many people in an enclosed space, good hygiene was the only way to prevent illness spreading throughout the ship. Pavel really should've known better than to leave his health to chance.

'I was going to, once we'd prepped for lunch. I thought it was too much drink but it hurts.' With that, he doubled over and vomited.

'Appendix?' Sophie suggested.

'Entirely possible. We need to get him down for tests right away.' The location of the pain, the fever and vomiting all pointed towards appendicitis, something that couldn't be left to chance. They would have to test his blood for signs of infection and X-ray his abdomen to confirm his diagnosis but he was certain that was what they were dealing with here.

Sophie commandeered one of the returning wheelchairs on his behalf and between them and the porter they got Pavel transferred into the chair.

'The crew lift is still working.' The porter pointed them in the right direction otherwise Luciano would have faced the prospect of carrying Pavel sedan chair–style down to the clinic.

'Thanks. We'll take him from here.' He didn't even have to ask Sophie if she was coming too.

Appendicitis often started with a dull cramping sensation. It was possible that the pain Pavel was experiencing meant the appendix was inflamed because it had been left too long without treatment. Usually they'd treat the condition with antibiotics until they reached the nearest port. Only blood tests and X-rays could tell him if his hunch was right and they were fast running out of time.

Despite being run off her feet with patients vying for her attention, Patrice provided a set of scrubs for Sophie to change into. 'Welcome on board.'

They mightn't have hit it off at the start when Sophie had questioned every aspect of Edith's treatment but she certainly looked relieved to have the extra help now. No wonder. The waiting room and corridors were chock-a-block with injured passengers. Thankfully the lower decks had suffered minimal, superficial damage and there had been no major injuries reported so far. Hopefully those waiting would be patched up quickly and able to continue their holiday without too much disruption.

Luciano had already informed her that they needed to jump the X-ray queue as a matter of urgency, so he'd gone ahead, leaving Sophie to change in his office. Their earlier almost-kiss seemed like a lifetime ago now. Those fevered bodies entwined in this very room a short time ago had been doused with cold water even before the wave had hit.

Yet he'd gone after her. Why? When Luciano had been the one saying it was wrong and there was no future for them? He'd saved her too. He'd caught her with so much conviction he could've broken a rib. Now wasn't the time to get into it but when the ship was calm again, she intended to stir the waters with him. She wasn't going to drift away without a fight.

As soon as she'd changed and pulled her damp hair into a more manageable ponytail, she sought her place beside Luciano in one of the treatment rooms.

'Do you want the bad news or the worse news?' He pulled her to one side, with Pavel's X-rays to hand.

Her stomach plummeted. She had hoped the tests would prove them wrong and he'd simply been suffering from an easily treated urinary tract infection. Appendicitis on a ship in bad weather wasn't as straightforward as it might have been in a hospital.

'His appendix?'

'Ruptured.' He was right, that was the

worst possible scenario. Life-threatening. A ruptured appendix could spread the infection into the bloodstream and could be fatal if emergency surgery wasn't performed to remove it and clean the abdominal cavity.

'We need to get him to hospital for surgery at the next port, then?' The hospital would be better equipped to perform the procedure than the medical centre, which was essentially an infirmary, not a hospital.

'We do but we don't know when that's going to take place due to the weather. According to the captain, we're too far out to have Pavel evacuated by helicopter and the weather is too bad to make it into port any time soon. I need to move now.'

'You're going to operate?'

'I don't see that we have any choice. We can't wait for sepsis to set in.'

'You're sure you're not rushing into this?' It wasn't that she doubted his medical opinion but this sounded too close to home. He'd told her he'd lost his wife to sepsis and was still reeling from the consequences of that. If he had another patient succumb he might never recover from it. She would go along with whatever decision he made but in this case she wanted him to be doubly sure he was doing the right thing.

'You think I'd put a patient's life at risk simply to justify my own existence? To prove I could've saved my wife if I'd acted sooner? I already know that, Sophie. Trust me, that's something my conscience won't let me forget. Oh, and to put your mind further at ease, the captain is in agreement that this is the best course of action in such life-threatening circumstances.' He was trying and failing to control the volume of his voice, every inch of him as tense as a coiled cobra ready to strike.

It was understandable when she'd insulted his capacity as a medic and an honourable man.

'I had to ask, Luciano,' she mumbled, wondering if that was true or if she'd simply wanted to know for herself if he was truly over the manner in which his wife had passed. It was becoming more and more difficult for her to keep her distance from him, emotionally as well as physically. She didn't want to cross that line with him if he was still confused about what he wanted. It would only cause him more heartache in the long run and she didn't want to put him through that simply because she fancied him.

'It's a question I've already asked myself but I always put my patients first. He can't, *we* can't, wait any longer. The coastguard and closest hospital are on standby but this is an emergency. Believe it or not, we're equipped to deal with those.'

'I understand that. I wasn't trying to undermine you or the facilities here.'

'I should hope not. Along with speaking English, cruise doctors have to be able to perform advanced life-support practices, emergency cardiovascular care and minor surgical procedures.'

'I worked as a theatre nurse for a while. I can assist.' His eyebrows shot up. 'What? You're not the only one who had a working life outside this ship.'

He shook his head. 'You're always surprising me, Sophie, that's all.'

She didn't know what that meant other than that he'd never asked about her previous work experience and vice versa. All they really knew about each other was based on their time together during this trip. It had proved enough for her to let Luciano close but she wasn't sure he was ready to let her in.

With the anaesthetic administered, it was time to do what Luciano did best: work under pressure. In contrast to his time working in the hospital, he hadn't been tested too often during his time at sea. Usually the priority was keeping the patient stabilised until they could reach land. However, they weren't unused to dealing with emergencies. Getting the coastguard out to evacuate a patient by helicopter was rare. Not only did it put vulnerable patients at risk, it could be dangerous for the crew and everyone on board. It was strictly limited to emergencies and better weather.

They had a small operating room with the equipment to carry out one of the most common emergency abdominal surgeries. But Luciano was finding it difficult not to consider the implications of the appendix having already burst, especially when he'd lost his own wife to a blood infection.

'Scalpel.'

Sophie handed him the instrument and he made the first incision into Pavel's stomach, cold sweat beginning to form all over his body.

It had been some time since he'd done anything like this and there was a lot riding on the outcome—not least his burden of guilt. He couldn't lose anyone else this way. Certainly not if Sophie believed he was doing this to somehow make up for his wife's death. It was precisely the opposite.

His growing feelings towards Sophie led him to believe he was finally moving out of his mourning period. He'd never forget Renata or what had happened but life had to continue without her. That was what scared him. Not knowing what the future held or if he'd lose someone else.

Death could happen in an instant. If they hadn't acted so quickly with Pavel he could've died. He still might. Life was a fragile thing. But so was Luciano's heart. He wasn't sure it would withstand losing someone else he loved. It was that fear that kept him from getting too involved with anyone else.

'Dr Montavano? Luciano?' Sophie registered his hesitation but he was confident in his medical skills. It was fate that unnerved him. All the expertise in the world couldn't help if events like this were predetermined. Perhaps the wave had happened so they would come to Pavel's aid in time. Perhaps Renata was always going to die, no matter what he did or didn't do. In which case, it made a mockery of his attempts to avoid any emotional entanglements. There was no way to outrun destiny and only a fool would try. Sophie standing here beside him was proof. They kept being thrown together—sometimes literally. These were all signs he should stop fighting his feelings and just let fate take its course.

'I…er… I am just going to divide the fat and underlying tissue to expose the site.'

'Yes, Doctor.' Sophie helped with the positioning of the self-retaining retractors to hold the tissue out of the way so he could work freely.

He did a finger sweep to locate the appendix before carefully tying off both ends. With precise movements he dissected it and disposed of it into the tray Sophie held out to him.

'I need to irrigate the abdomen.' It was necessary to eliminate any bacterial contamination to prevent septicaemia by flushing out the area with saline. Once it was all drained away again, and he had checked the gall bladder and liver to make sure they hadn't been affected during the procedure, he was able to begin closing the wound.

To Luciano, suturing was a signal that he'd completed his task and he could begin to relax. It was something he had plenty of experience doing on board. There was no shortage of gashed knees around the pool or drunken passengers cut by broken glasses they'd dropped.

'We'll leave the drainage tube in to make sure all infection is clear and keep him on antibiotics and painkillers for a few days.'

'How long do you think it will take for him to recover?'

'It will probably take a few weeks to get back to full health. Hopefully most of that will be done in a hospital.'

When the crisis had been averted and Pavel had been sewn up again, Luciano breathed a bigger sigh of relief than he'd ever done in a hospital emergency department.

'Thanks for your assistance, Nurse Blythe.' She'd been a quiet, calming presence beside him, assisting his progress with her physical support and a quiet confidence in his abilities.

'Any time, Dr Montavano. It was my privilege to work with you. You saved his life. You should be proud of yourself.' Only Sophie's eyes were visible above her face mask but they expressed genuine respect for him.

'No, *we* did and I think we deserve a drink after that.' Today had been a wake-up call. Life was too short and, as he knew all too well, could be snuffed out at any time. He couldn't spend the rest of his life worrying and grieving when every second was too precious to waste. Instead of trying to quash his feelings towards Sophie, he should be celebrating the fact that he'd met someone who'd resurrected the side of him he'd thought had died with Renata.

'Are you allowed to socialise with the riff-raff? Isn't there a danger you'll get mobbed? You're the closest thing to a celebrity around here.' She was mocking him but he didn't care when she made him laugh so easily. Even if nothing happened between them, he enjoyed being around her. He didn't need to keep punishing himself by remaining in isolation.

'I was thinking about the crew bar. You're a member of staff now.'

'Ah, so it's just a drink between two work colleagues after a difficult day?'

'What else would it be?' He didn't see any reason to label it as something else in case it didn't work out or scared her off. She knew about his past and his current confusion. It would be understandable if she didn't want to get involved in his mess when all she was looking for was a bit of fun on holiday.

'You're right. It'll be nothing more than two people meeting at the same time in the same place, socialising outside work.' Her teasing made it evident she didn't believe it

CHAPTER EIGHT

'NOT A DATE,' Sophie reminded herself in the full-length mirror at the end of the bed. Luciano had told her exactly that when they'd made the arrangement.

It didn't matter that her body was burning for more or that his vocal protest hadn't matched his body language. He was still in mourning and therefore it didn't make any sense to keep a candle burning for him. She'd only get burned. Besides, after-work drinks with a colleague was still more of a social life than she'd had in a long time.

There was a rap on the door.

'Not a date,' she reiterated. Yeah, right. That was why she'd showered, blow-dried her hair, put make-up on and dressed to impress.

On her way to answer the door her heart gave an unprompted leap, trying to escape the confines of her chest. Why did the pros-any more than he did and there was a chink of hope that it wasn't too late to act.

'I trust I'll have to go and get changed. Unless it's some sort of fancy-dress theme we're going for?'

'I'll come by your cabin at about eight.' He had no choice but to accompany her when he'd have to practically smuggle her in. It was a risk taking her into crew quarters, even if she was a temporary recruit, but he was willing to do it if it meant he could spend more time with her.

'All right. It's a date,' she said blowing him a kiss as she left and almost sending him into cardiac arrest.

pect of spending the night with Luciano seem more intimidating than assisting him with emergency surgery?

She forced herself into an I'm-not-bothered-at-all casual stance as she opened the door… until she saw him leaning against the door frame in his black turtleneck and dark grey chinos. Cartoon-style *Arooga!* signs went off in her head and she imagined her eyes had popped out on stalks. He'd shaved and his hair had that fluffy, just-washed look, and he smelled divine—of citrus and the sea. Forbidden fruit and freedom.

'Hey.' She suddenly felt very shy.

It might've had something to do with the way he was looking at her. As though the royal blue silk jumpsuit Edith had talked her into buying 'for one of those fancy dinners they do with the captain' was the disposable wrapper on a sweet he was about to devour. It was not an unwanted reaction and perhaps exactly what she'd been hoping for when she'd chosen the outfit tonight.

'Too much? Not enough?'

The longer he took to reply the more room there was for the doubt crows to set up roost.

It was way too many rapid heartbeats until he answered, 'Just right.'

'Just call me Goldilocks.' She flicked

her hair off her shoulder with the sass of a woman who knew she could have anything she wanted—including the sexy man at her door.

'I thought you might like to go for dinner first. Have you eaten?'

'Not yet.' Her stomach had been in too much turmoil at the prospect of spending the evening with Luciano to contemplate eating a meal. Now she was glad she'd waited. It would line her stomach before they went for drinks but it would also give them more time together.

'Dinner it is, then.' He offered her his arm and she hooked her own through it as they made their way through the corridors into the glitz of the atrium, where the awe-inspiring chandelier hanging from the ceiling seemed to illuminate every deck and the glass staircase glittered with encrusted crystals.

'Wait, doesn't dinner lead us into date territory?' There could be little doubt about what was happening now but she liked teasing him. He'd told her he hadn't as much as looked at anyone whilst in mourning so taking someone out for dinner wouldn't be an everyday occurrence for him. Or her.

'We don't have to label this as anything.

Let's just go with the flow, Sophie.' He seemed much more at ease about going out as he adopted her recent philosophy; it brought a smile to both of their faces.

'Are we going to one of those posh restaurants? I suppose you can get a table any time you choose. The rest of us mere mortals have to join a waiting list before we can gain admittance.'

As they strolled arm in arm past the queues of people outside the Japanese and French restaurants, she admitted to feeling smug. She'd had her time as a solo diner and not only was she in the company of the most handsome man on board but one of the most important. Even out of uniform he drew nods of respect from those around him. He took it all in his stride but Sophie took it as the measure of the man as much as the doctor that he was appreciated and liked by all. Including her.

'I thought we'd go somewhere more exclusive.' Bypassing all the other guests, he took her towards the lift and pressed the 'up' button. They were the only ones in the lift but the atmosphere between them was buzzing with expectation for the evening that lay ahead.

Perhaps the crew had a separate restaurant

and he had a chef friend who was going to cook specially for them.

When they arrived on the now-familiar deck and walked towards the all-day buffet, that fizz of excitement suddenly went flat. She was aware that everyone else who was walking around, plates in hand, helping themselves to the array of food, were dressed very casually. Shorts, T-shirts and sundresses were the uniform here, and she was distinctly out of place. The eyes assessing her outfit told her so.

'I think I'm a tad overdressed. I wish you'd told me this was what you had in mind.' It didn't matter to her where they went when Luciano's company was the main attraction but by building her hopes for something fabulous he'd left room for disappointment.

'We're not there yet. Don't worry. You look amazing.' He gave her a squeeze but she was only reassured when they carried on past the main dining area and down a flight of stairs.

The restaurant below was small, intimate, with a distinctly French theme. The decor was cream and black with paintings of fruit and old wine caskets dotted around to give it some colour and texture. It would've been perfect if not for the fact that it was empty and the chairs were stacked on the tables.

'You did tell them we were coming, didn't you? Or are we too early?' There weren't even any staff about so goodness knew when dinner was going to be served.

'I called in a favour. Come with me.' He took her by the hand and led her past the closed bar and serving area towards the door marked *Staff Only*. With a flick of a light switch he revealed a spotless kitchen.

'Ta-da!'

Sophie looked at the empty stainless-steel surfaces then back at him. 'Ta-da, what? I don't understand what I'm supposed to be looking at.'

'We have free rein to make our own dinner here. This is ours for the night. They only use this as an overflow during lunchtimes.'

She got why this might be a big deal for him when he'd spent the last eight months having meals made for him. It was a novelty. To her, though, not cooking every night was a bonus of this holiday.

'Great. What are we doing? Reheating leftovers?' She couldn't muster a whole lot of enthusiasm with a rumbling stomach. Perhaps they should've grabbed a plate on the way through the buffet and come down here to eat in peace instead.

Luciano cocked his head to one side and watched her with amusement. 'No. I'm going to cook for you.'

Now, that changed things. Made it more intimate. Special. He wanted to cook for her and this was as close as she'd get to him taking her back to his place. The equivalent to a fourth or fifth date in her mind. What else would you call leaving the public arena, letting her into his inner sanctum, and trying to impress her with his culinary skills?

'What are we having?'

'Pasta.'

'Oh.' Her anticipation of watching him show off in the kitchen as expertly as he'd done in the operating room was quashed as quickly as it had sprung up. Even she could throw a bag of pasta into some boiling water. She tried to look on the bright side. Whatever the meal, they were getting to spend some time together.

He pulled out a stool and rolled up his sleeves. 'If you want to sit there, I'll get started.'

She sat down while he flitted about the kitchen, gathering ingredients. He opened the fridge and loaded his arms with fresh produce. Which, frankly, she thought was overkill when he could easily open a jar. Then he dropped an onion on the floor and bent down to retrieve it, giving her the opportunity to ogle…and she was definitely grateful for the view.

'Do you do this often? Take over the kitchen?'

He set the food on the counter before reaching for two wine glasses out of the dishwasher. 'Never. I cook at home, or I used to. This is the first time I've commandeered the galley.'

'The first time? I'm privileged.'

'I've been saving this too.' He uncorked a bottle of wine. 'It's from the family vineyard. I had to smuggle this on board with me.'

'Are you sure you want to waste that on me?' She was honoured he deemed her special enough to crack open the bottle after all this time but she wasn't sure she deserved it.

'It's not a waste when I'm sharing it in good company.' He poured two glasses and handed one to her.

'I suppose it beats drinking it by yourself in your room. To good company.' She clinked her glass to his in a toast then took a sip of the mellow red liquid. It tasted of summer and carefree afternoons in the sun somewhere she wished they were able to visit together.

'Tastes as good as I remember. Like home.' For someone who claimed he had been desperate to escape the place he appeared wistful at the reminder.

'It's really nice but I imagine we shouldn't drink too much of it on an empty stomach.'

'Is that a hint to get on with cooking your dinner?'

'Not at all. I'm simply saying if we don't eat soon I might end up dancing on the tables and singing like a scalded cat.'

'Okay, okay. I'll get started.' He opened more cupboards until he found the dry ingredients he was looking for. 'Although, I wouldn't mind seeing that.'

'Cook,' she said, rapping her knuckles on the work surface.

'*Si, signorina.*'

Sophie watched as he poured out some flour, made a well in the centre and cracked eggs into the middle of it. 'I thought we were having pasta?'

'We are. I'm making it now. No self-respecting Italian would ever use that dried rubbish. We only use fresh, home-made pasta.' He started mixing the concoction with a fork and added a dash of salt.

'You're making your own pasta? Right now?' The idea was incomprehensible to her when to most people it was a convenience food made in minutes. Still, she appreciated the effort.

'It's not a big deal.' He was kneading the dough, bringing it together into a ball with a smooth action. The few times she'd tried to make dough it had been a sticky mess, clinging to her hands, the work surfaces and the rolling pin, bearing no resemblance to the pictures in the recipe book.

'It is to me. I can't remember the last time I cooked a proper meal. There doesn't seem any point for one person. Usually I make do with some beans on toast. Sometimes I change it up with some cheese too. I suppose all Italians learn to cook at their mamma's knee?'

'Something like that. Everything was centred around our kitchen at home. It's the most important room in the house.' After he'd stretched the dough out a few times, he flattened it on the counter with the rolling pin.

'I need to let that rest for a while,' he said, then set to work chopping and frying off the vegetables in a little olive oil. Once the sauce was simmering away on the stove, he pulled out some sort of steel trap.

'What's that? Some kind of torture device?'

'It's to make the pasta. Have you never used one?'

'I've never even seen one before.' She got up to inspect this strange toy he was completely at ease with.

'Would you like to try?'

'I don't want to ruin anything.'

'You can't. It's fine. Hold this and I'll fetch you an apron. I wouldn't want you to ruin your outfit.' He left her in charge of his creation to get something to cover her clothes. In hindsight, silk wasn't the best choice for working in the kitchen.

He hung the apron around her neck then leaned in to double tie it around her waist. He was so close she could feel his breath at her neck and all the way down to her toes. 'Thanks.'

'We feed the dough in here and wind the handle to flatten it out. See?' With his head at her shoulder, his chest to her back, he guided her hands with his to make the dough into a smooth sheet.

'Uh huh?' She wasn't paying any attention to what he was showing her, only what he was doing to her by being so close.

'Your turn,' he said, testing her. She'd have done a better job of telling him what aftershave he was wearing or what tooth-paste he'd used because she'd paid more at-tention to those details.

As a result, she was all fingers and thumbs, her composure in tatters from hav-ing him touch her. His lovely pasta dough got caught up in the machine and fell out in lumps instead of the smooth sheet he'd shown her.

'Sorry. I should've left it to the profes-sional.' She stood back, leaving him to clear up her mess and try to rectify it.

'Honestly, I haven't done this in ages. I think the last time I did this was for… It doesn't matter. It's all done now anyway.' He expertly whizzed it back through the steel mangle a few times before producing freshly cut spaghetti.

'It's all right. You can say her name. We've both been as churned up as my at-tempt at using the pasta machine because of our pasts. You don't have to hide it and there's no point in pretending the worst parts of our lives didn't happen.' Sophie took her seat again, content to let him chop the vegetables in case she lost a finger too.

It didn't bother her that he'd done this for his wife. On the contrary, she was glad he was sharing this side of himself with her. Clearly, he was comfortable enough with her to revisit something that meant a lot to him and held lots of memories—something of the life he'd run away from.

He kept winding the dough through until it was a long, silky ribbon. With the last pass through the machine, he cut it into thin strips. 'Renata. Cooking for her is one of the good memories I have. Sometimes they get lost in amongst the bad. The majority of our lives at the end revolved around tragedy. Now, do you want to set one of the tables in there or shall we eat here?'

Whilst a candlelit dinner in an otherwise empty restaurant would've been the traditionally more romantic option, she was content to be here, talking and getting him to open up to her.

'I'm happy to stay here.' She pulled a stool over for Luciano and once he'd cooked the pasta, he plated up the meals so they could eat together off the countertop he'd just cleaned.

'It's not quite the evening I had planned,' he said as he topped up their wine glasses.

'I'm still enjoying it, though, and this is delicious. You can definitely taste the difference with it being home-made.' Sophie did her best to twirl her spaghetti without splashing sauce over everything and completely showing herself up. Thank goodness for the giant bib she was wearing.

'*Buono.*'

'I don't think Ryan ever cooked for me. Not like this. He wined and dined me when we first got together but soon it was takeaways and comfortable nights in. By the end of the relationship we weren't eating together at all. He was always working late. Allegedly. He was probably out wooing his future wife. He left me with a few trust issues and called my judgement into question. I think that's why I was so defensive when we first met.'

'I'm not surprised. Although I think he's the one with the problem if he didn't appreciate what he already had at home. You're better off without him.'

'Yes, I am. It put me off the notion of men altogether.'

'And now?'

'I'm coming around to the idea again.'

Was it her imagination or were they flirting during this little heart-to-heart? She was afraid to call it that but there was definitely something springing to life between them again.

'I know what you mean. It was different with Renata and I. There was no cheating or Vegas wedding involved but I didn't think there'd be anyone after her.'

'And now?'

'I'm coming around to the idea.' His coy smile was as intoxicating as the wine she was sipping.

'I just couldn't face that kind of pain again. All our hopes for the future had been won and lost with the first pregnancy. After she lost the baby, having another became an obsession. We both wanted a family and it became our sole focus. Our carefree life as a couple was over and all we cared about was seeing another positive pregnancy test. If I'd known I would lose her too I would've done things differently. We should've made the most of every second we had together.'

'How far along was she when you lost the baby?' Sophie's voice was barely a whisper, afraid to appear unsympathetic or obtrusive in the face of Luciano's heartbreak, but she wanted to get to know him and understand his state of mind.

'Only a few weeks the first time. Three months the second time. We'd already had the scan, heard the heartbeat and dared to believe we were going to be a family. Ten days later I'd lost them both. It took a long time for what had happened to sink in.'

'Shock, I suppose. You never expect something like that to happen. I'm so sorry, Luciano. My feckless ex doesn't even compare to what you've lost.'

'We've both suffered but I think the clouds are beginning to clear. I moved on from shock to grief and I think by signing on with the cruise company I moved into denial. Away from home and a life without Renata I was avoiding facing what had happened.'

'How do you feel about things now?' *About me?* she wanted to add, but this wasn't supposed to be about her. Luciano was sharing the very personal details of the worst time in his life. Something he hadn't discussed with anyone else. She was honoured that he was choosing to work through his emotions about that time with her.

He exhaled a long breath that seemed to come from deep within his soul. 'Honestly? I'm not one hundred percent sure. The thought of inviting more potential heartache into my life is terrifying. So is the thought of remaining alone for the rest of my life. Spending time with you has made me realise that.'

'Just take one step at a time. There's no need to rush into anything you're not ready for.'

He nodded. 'This is good. Just hanging out.'

'Do you know what I'm ready for now? Dessert!' It was clear they were both nursing old wounds, unwilling to commit to anything serious that would cause them to reopen old wounds, but at least they were acknowledging that. Sophie didn't want them to dig so deep that they became maudlin when their objective tonight was to have some fun together. They needed to get their date back on track.

'What would you like? I'm sure I could make something.'

'No. You do the dishes and I'll sort dessert.' It was her turn to surprise him, even if she was planning on taking a rather unconventional route.

When Luciano had cleaned up and come

to see what she was doing at the other end of the kitchen, he burst out laughing.

'That's cheating,' he said as she started up the ice-cream machine.

'I didn't know there were rules. If you don't want me to...' She turned away and pretended to put one of the ice-cream cones back in the box.

'I didn't say that. Please may I have an ice-cream cone too?'

Sophie pulled the lever until the nozzle piped a frilly mixture of chocolate and vanilla dairy goodness into both cones. 'Why don't we go up on deck and take these with us?'

She wasn't ready for the night to end and she hoped he felt the same way.

There was an open-air movie screening near the bow of the ship, so Luciano directed Sophie towards the quieter end at the back. He was pleased she'd suggested this, otherwise he would've had to take her to one of the crew bars to continue their evening, and that would have meant sharing her. And, even worse, shouting about their feelings over the loud music within earshot of his crew mates.

He liked it being just the two of them. That was what had prompted him to make dinner himself and keep the evening intimate. He'd wanted quality time with Sophie, time and space to express their fears about what was developing between them. Neither of them was going to jump into something serious and Sophie wasn't pressuring him for anything. He didn't need to be on his guard around her. She had become a symbol of everything that would be available to him in the future.

'It's quiet here. I like it.' Sophie was peering over the side of the ship as she finished her ice cream, watching the wake left in the waves.

Luciano moved over beside her and rested his arms on the rail. 'That's because everything's closed until tomorrow. There's no reason for anyone to come this way. Sometimes I come here at night for a timeout.'

During the day this area was heaving, mostly with children, for use of the climbing wall and the waterslide. For safety reasons they shut down before sun set. He preferred it when the rows of redundant sunbeds were stacked and the sound of the sea replaced the noise of shrieking.

'A timeout from what? Being on your own?' Sophie laughed at her own joke and he decided he preferred that over all other sounds.

'I suppose I have become something of a hermit.' He tossed the last of his cone overboard and watched as it disappeared into the darkness.

'A hermit in plain sight of thousands of passengers and crew. That's quite a feat.'

'Yet you're the only one to notice.' Of all the people he'd met, of all the friends he'd made, Sophie was the only one who'd gotten close enough to see he was essentially alone. It said a lot about her and how much he thought of her to let her in.

'Birds of a feather and all that.' Sometimes an English turn of phrase went beyond his knowledge of the language.

'Pardon?' He looked up at the sky, trying to figure out what she was talking about, but he couldn't even see any seagulls about.

'Oh, Luciano.' Her giggle was a glorious sound, even if it had come at his expense, but it was the hand lightly resting on his chest that he took most pleasure in. 'It simply means we're very alike. I've spent a lot of time on my own too.'

'Not tonight, though.'

'No. Not tonight. I've enjoyed the company very much.' Sophie faced him and he found he was jealous of the moon putting the silver sparkle in her eyes and the tongue that had licked the last of the ice cream from her lips.

'Me too.' With every word they uttered they were gradually moving closer to each other. No longer fighting the inevitable but fully embracing it.

She tilted her chin up towards him and, convinced this was what he and Sophie both wanted, he captured her mouth with his in a ferocious expression of his desire for her.

Her hand, previously resting on his chest, was clutching the back of his neck. He pulled her forcefully to him, his hands sliding along the cool silk at her back. Everything she'd inspired in him tonight was wrapped up in that kiss. A wish to move on, to live again and enjoy being with someone free from guilt.

Any second now Sophie was sure she'd wake up. This had to be a dream. It was the only explanation as to why she'd found herself here under the moonlight with a gorgeous Italian kissing her as though his life depended on it. All the promises she'd made to herself to steer clear of men launched themselves overboard with the first touch of his lips against hers. There was no sane reason to deny herself this taste of passion.

Luciano couldn't do to her what Ryan had done. He had no intention of marrying anyone and she was the one who'd be doing the leaving in a matter of days. There could be no misunderstanding of their relationship or time to resent each other when every moment together was precious and getting hotter by the second.

The heat of his touch was scorching her skin, sending arousal coursing through her like molten lava. His tongue was rough against hers, and insistent. The firm pressure of his mouth, wrapped up in the warmth of his embrace, was enough to make a girl go weak at the knees. Thankfully, Luciano took the strain, lifting her up against the rail so she could wrap herself around him.

'Go for it, mate!'

'Put her down!'

'Twit-twoo!'

Drunken jeers and wolf whistles ended their clinch all too soon, neither of them wanting to be entertainment for drunken passers-by.

'Let's get out of here.' Luciano took her hand, his face dark and tense whilst she was sure hers was scarlet at being caught smooching in a very public display of affection.

The sound carried down the stairs with them.

'Idiots.' They'd spoiled their evening with their childish taunts because it soon became obvious Luciano was escorting her back to her cabin. Date over.

'I'm sorry if I embarrassed you. I should've known better than to kiss you where people could see.' As they reached her door all his good humour seemed to have dissipated thanks to the interruption.

'You didn't embarrass me. I was just sorry it ended. Do you want to come in and pick up where we left off?' Sophie opened the door as she made the bold invitation. By putting herself out there she knew she was risking rejection but this was what she wanted. There was no way she was going home with regrets. She had enough of those already. Luciano was her new start and that meant being honest with herself.

She recognised the flare of interest darken Luciano's eyes seconds prior to his mouth securely imprisoning hers. She wasn't going to attempt to break free when this was all she'd dreamed of since that last kiss had robbed her of her senses.

Luciano held her face in his hands, kissing her as though it might be for the last time, and backed her farther into her room. She barely had time to register the implication of the move when he kicked the door shut behind them. This was really happening.

'I guess this was a date after all.' She was breathless as she tugged at his shirt, wanting him naked before he had time to change his mind again. He stopped kissing her long enough to strip it off for her then resumed his passionate exploration of her mouth.

She drew her hands over the expanse of his broad chest, exploring the contrast of rough hair and smooth skin beneath her fingertips.

'Unlike any I've ever had before,' he muttered, kissing the skin behind her ear then across her shoulder.

With an impressive sleight of hand, he undid her zip and peeled away her silk layer. Sophie let it fall around her feet and stepped out of it so she was standing before him in only her lingerie.

'What changed your mind about doing this?' Sophie's voice was breathy with anticipation as he undid her bra and brushed his thumbs across her budding nipples.

'We've only got one life. We should live

it to the fullest. Squeeze every drop out of it.' He plucked the sensitive nubs between his fingers with a glint in his eye that made her breath catch in her throat all over again. This matched up to every hot dream she'd ever had about Luciano.

She was standing there, exposed and vulnerable, shaking with nerves and need. Luciano didn't have any such qualms as he shifted down her body, his tongue zigzagging across her hyper-sensitive skin until he reached her belly, making her practically convulse with want for him. He hooked his fingers into either side of her panties and slid them infuriatingly slowly down her legs until he was kneeling at her feet and she was completely naked.

Luciano nudged her legs apart so she was open to him, anchored her with his hands at her waist and buried his face between her legs. The instant his tongue darted into her core she had to hold onto his shoulders in case she collapsed, the exquisite sensation rendering the rest of her body immobile. All of her focus was on that one area, proving exactly why Italians had a reputation as excellent lovers. He butterflied in and out of her, drinking her nectar with his fluttering tongue.

Somewhere beyond her closed eyelids and out-of-body feeling she heard the frantic gasps of a woman on the blink of oblivion and realised it was her. Her orgasm came hard and there was no stemming the shudders of ecstasy racking her body.

A determined Luciano didn't deviate in his pursuit of her complete satisfaction until she was breathless with exhaustion and her legs were quivering as she fought to remain upright. It was no wonder the French called it *la petite mort*, comparing the post-orgasm sensation to death. She thought she had died and gone to heaven a million times over.

Her chest was heaving as she fought to get her breathing back to normal, with Luciano kissing his way back up her torso.

'Oh, my. That was…' No words could describe what he'd done to her or how amazing it had been.

'We aren't finished yet.' He popped his fly open and the sound was even sexier than his laugh.

They tumbled onto her bed, with Luciano still nuzzling against her neck, caressing her breasts with his large hands and generally testing her limits.

He was all hard muscle and soft kisses lying on top of her and she wanted to fold him right into her body. Except there was that niggling voice of her conscience refusing to shut up about him not being ready for this. But when he brushed against her inner thigh, she knew he was more than ready.

His hot breath in her ear started another tremor throughout her already satiated body. He entered her quickly, stretching and filling her all at once, and her gasp was drowned out by Luciano's groan. It was good to know she wasn't the only one finding this overwhelming.

He gave her a shaky smile before pressing another kiss on her lips, his eyes filled with a dazed look that showed he was experiencing the same thing she was. When he began moving inside her she knew it was the beginning of something out of this world.

It wasn't long before her exhausted body sprang back to life, greedy for more, urging Luciano to take her back to that heady paradise again. As she tightened around him, the pace between them increased to fever pitch, both desperate to reach that release and the promise of bliss. He was like a drug to her now, every hit pushing reality further away and making her want this to last for ever.

'Sophie.' He cried out her name at the height of his climax, pulling her with him.

Together they toppled over the precipice, breathless but happy when they finally came back down to earth.

Despite the air-conditioning, Sophie was perspiring from the heat they'd generated.

'So much for the shower I had.'

Luciano lay beside her, continuing to map her body with his hands and mouth. 'Are you complaining, *mi amore*?'

'Not. At. All.'

He cupped her breast and took her nipple in his mouth, sucking until she was straddling the line that bordered pain and pleasure.

'Luciano... I need a breather.' She giggled, exertion taking its toll after so many years of celibacy.

'Sorry. I just can't get enough of you.' His need was growing steadily against her by the second.

They were the words every woman wanted to hear. Yet Sophie couldn't help but interpret them with some trepidation.

In a matter of days this was all going to be over. It wasn't simply the euphoria of being post-orgasm, she wanted more of this, more of him. Why did she always fall for the wrong man? Or the right man at the wrong time? If she'd met him during the freedom years she might have joined him on the cruise life and had a series of adventures. As it was, she had a job and a mortgage to return to while Luciano was rediscovering his zest for life. Without her. That made her sadder than anything.

For now, she wanted to stay in this loved-up bubble of a holiday romance where anything was possible. They didn't have much time left together before she had to go back to reality. Like all the best vacations, she never wanted this to end.

'What's stopping you from taking what you want?' Her words came out of the bravado of a woman who wanted a lifetime of memories to take back to England. She was lying naked, coyly batting her eyelashes, whilst her hand was straying down his chest, his taut stomach and towards his solid arousal.

He gave another groan but the expression on his face was one of pure pleasure. 'I thought you needed a breather?'

'I'm breathing. See?' She drew in a few exaggerated breaths delighted in his lustful eyes watching her breasts rise and fall.

With a territorial growl he rolled her onto her back and pinned her hands above her head. Her pulse spiked with anticipation and

s to straddle his hips. She was like a
ss, naked and wanting, and she was
s. For now.

en they were moving together, his
s at her waist as she ground against
he was in ecstasy. It wasn't only the sex
was great, they had a real connection
never thought he'd have with anyone
There didn't seem to be a logical rea-
to let her disappear out of his life. Once
tepped off this ship they weren't likely
to cross paths again. If these past years
taught him anything, it was to savour
ood times with loved ones because you
r knew when it could all come crashing
. In this instance he knew the date he'd
Sophie. This time he could do some-
g to prevent his heart from being broken.
was easy to say 'live in the moment' and
pt what they had for now, but the mo-
t was almost over. He was done being
ive. Now was the time to be proactive.
he'd told him she wasn't happy with her
in England and he was almost ready to
ome again. Given the chance, Sophie
ld love his part of Italy. She wanted to
el. It was up to him to let her know that
an option because he'd spent so long
ng her he wasn't ready to move on again.

awareness that he could do anything to her
he chose. And that she trusted him not to do
anything to hurt her.

'What is this spell you've cast over me,
Sophie? You're all I think about. All I want.'
There was such genuine confusion in his
voice that she felt guilty about distracting
him from the grief he'd clung to.

'I'm sorry.' Tears pooled in her eyes. She'd
been selfish. Only thinking about herself
and her needs when Luciano had told her
he wasn't ready for another relationship. No
matter how short-lived.

He frowned at her and released her from
his hold. 'Don't ever be sorry for who you
are. You've done nothing except remind me
I'm alive.'

His kiss was sweet and tender and made
her cry all the more. When they joined their
bodies together once again, making love
slowly this time, she knew the tears had been
of self-pity. She'd fallen for him, but in only
a few days she'd have to let him go and return to her responsibilities. This couldn't be
any more than a holiday fling, and that was
never going to be enough for her.

Luciano had forgotten what it was to wake
up lying in bed beside someone. Disoriented

at first, he wondered why he was so warm and why he couldn't move. He opened his eyes to see Sophie's naked body wrapped around his. Rather than pulling away, he snuggled in closer. Her soft breath against his skin and her arm draped possessively around his midriff were things he could get used to. He'd found the peace of mind and joy in his life that he'd been searching for since losing Renata. She was always going to have a special place in his heart, but so was Sophie.

She'd shown him how important it was to receive support as well as give it. Made him see he was allowed to have fun, to explore everything the world had to offer without having to feel guilty about it. Taught him to live the life he was lucky to have. Most of all, she'd taught him to open his heart again. He'd taken the next step with Sophie because he was ready for it, ready to let someone into his life again.

She was sleeping soundly on his chest, unaware of the revelations going on inside him. Sophie had opened up a whole new world to him, one outside his grief and the ship. The problem was she was leaving in a couple of days. That was why it was more important than ever to stop denying himself the right

to be happy again. Even if short time.

He brushed his fingers t letting the silky tresses fal She stirred beneath his tou

'Is everything okay?' sh eyes closed, her arm still v his torso. He didn't want thi tempted to close his eyes ag to sleep.

Unfortunately, he couldr that just yet. 'I'm going to h to my own cabin, *mia cara*.'

'It's the middle of the nigl

'I can't risk anyone seeing of a passenger's cabin in the

'I thought I was staff now circle around his nipple with trying to distract him…and s

'It would look bad for the c don't approve of relationships members either.'

'We have a few hours left No one's going to see you.' Sh feathery kisses across his che impossible for him to leave no

'Uh-huh? What have you got then?'

'I can think of a few things.' S

acros
godd
all hi
W
hand
him,
that
he'd
else.
son
she
ever
had
the
nev
dow
lose
thin
It
acc
me
pas
S
life
go
wo
tra
wa
tell

They could sort something out if they wanted this to work. After being on his own for so long, he knew he could do a long-distance relationship if it came to it. As long as he knew he'd get to do this with Sophie again, he'd survive.

He'd talk to her tomorrow when they were able to think more clearly. The things she was currently doing to him made Luciano feel as though his brain was about to explode, along with every other part of him. He thrust his hips up, plunging deeper, faster inside her until she was tightening around him, her hands clawing at his chest as she rode to climax with him.

The one thing he was sure of was that he was going to make the most of their time together in case it was their last. He sure as hell wanted to give Sophie reason to remember him, if not come to the same conclusion he had. That what they had together was worth more than a mere fling.

CHAPTER NINE

IT WAS CANNES TODAY. Sophie had never been to France and was looking forward to visiting the most romantic country in the world with her lover. Unlike her, however, Luciano was working. Now they were in port, he'd had to oversee patient transfers to the nearest hospital and was responsible for follow-up appointments for those who had injuries from the rogue wave. She could've undertaken this excursion on her own but had chosen to wait for him to join her. It was strange how quickly she'd become used to being part of a couple.

It wasn't necessarily a good thing when she was going home at the end of the week and this trip was supposed to have been about finding herself again. Getting involved with a man hadn't been part of her plan. Edith's perhaps. She'd be over the moon to discover Sophie had had an affair in her absence.

They'd had only one night together thus far, but one that had left her throat raw from her very vocal orgasms and afraid to run into anyone from the neighbouring suites.

'*Je voudrais*...that one,' she said in her pitiful pidgin French that would have made her high-school French teacher weep.

There were a variety of vendors lined up along the harbour wall to greet disembarking passengers with hats and handbags for sale. She'd chosen a floppy white hat, which should do the job of shielding her from the morning sun and hopefully give her a touch of Riviera glamour appropriate for the trip.

'Let me get it for you,' Luciano insisted, and she was sure he handed over more than it actually cost.

A few euros lighter and one hat heavier, they made their way along the seafront. Wearing her black-and-white swing dress and shades, she liked to think she was channelling her inner Audrey Hepburn to fit in with the sophisticated surroundings. Luciano would make a handsome co-star who would've fitted in perfectly amongst Hollywood leading men like Cary Grant or Gregory Peck.

Last night had surprised her in more ways than she could possibly have imagined. It was so unfair that she couldn't have that passion in her life for ever. After a while it would fade, as she knew all too well, but that didn't stop her hoping it was possible to maintain that level of passion in a relationship. Sadly, life with Ryan had shown her otherwise. He'd decided the only way to recapture that intoxicating desire had been to find it with another woman.

Luciano would have to remain a lovely, sizzling memory because anything more would eventually turn into disappointment. She wasn't going to repeat history. Especially when she knew how much baggage he was carrying with him.

For now, she was an exciting distraction for him. Ultimately, he was a man who would want to settle down, replace the wife he'd lost and probably the family he'd been denied. He wouldn't find that with her.

That was what she was telling herself. She didn't know how she was going to manage to say goodbye. The thought of going home was more depressing than ever. It was hard enough swapping this relatively stress-free life in such a beautiful setting for her humdrum existence. Because that was all it was:

an existence. Out here she was properly living. And a lot of that was down to Luciano's company inside and outside the bedroom.

'It's a whole different world out here, isn't it?' Luciano echoed her thoughts about surroundings she'd only seen on TV before now.

'It doesn't seem like a real place, more like a playground for rich kids and tycoons.' You only had to take a glance up the road to see the souped-up sports cars or hear their modified engines to understand the kind of money that was thrown about here. It was interesting to see how the other half lived and pretend to be part of it for an afternoon.

'We can play here for a little while at least.'

'I wonder what it would be like to live here?'

'Permanently? Financially impossible, I would have thought.'

'I could always live on the beach. I think I could be happy there.'

'I don't doubt it, my little drifter.' He hugged her close, apparently comfortable enough outside the confines of the ship to show his affection towards her. She wasn't complaining and snuggled further into his arms. The nickname he'd given her was apt, she thought. It was more in keeping with the woman she wanted to rediscover—continually moving around without any fixed home or job. She was sure he meant it in the most endearing terms and not with any negative connotations. He got her.

Sophie stopped, stood up on tiptoe and kissed him full on the lips.

'Mmm… What was that for?' He lifted her sunglasses up so he could see into her eyes and kissed her back.

'For being you.' She liked the fact that he didn't shy away from her, even though they were in a public place. As if he no longer cared about the rules when he was with her. Even now there were faces she recognised walking by, the occasional greeting thrown their way. No one seemed to mind in the slightest about what they were doing and she liked to think that they looked so happy together no one would begrudge them this time together.

'We should go exploring. Perhaps we'll stumble onto a movie set somewhere.'

Sophie didn't think she could stand much more excitement today but all the shops and fabulous-looking buildings appeared to be uphill. She could spend all day walking along the shore with Luciano but it did seem a waste to be here and not see something of the sights.

'There's a park across the road. We could cut through there.' She spotted the little oasis of palm trees in the centre of the town and it seemed a good halfway point between the solace of the beach and the rest of the bustling resort.

They dodged through the traffic and entered the park through the black wrought-iron gate. It was like walking into another world. The palm trees lining the pathway provided some much-needed shade and the plots of greenery afforded a different kind of freshness than they'd found the shore.

'It's so peaceful in here.' Even Luciano seemed impressed by it. The gardens made a change from the sea view he was used to.

'We can sit a while if you'd like. There's a bench over in the corner.' They weren't in any rush to go anywhere and it would be nice to rest her feet for a while before they attempted to hike up the steep streets.

'I'd rather do that than join in with the group.' Luciano pointed at the visitors nearby, contorting themselves into shapes on the grass as part of what she assumed was a yoga class. She'd never taken part in one herself because she got all the exercise she needed being on her feet all day in the nursing home. Although she had always thought it did look calming for the soul. Something she would need when the day came that Luciano wasn't available to do the job.

They flopped down onto the bench and it felt natural for Sophie to cuddle up with him. Despite the noise from a few children in the playground nearby, it was peaceful. They could've been anywhere at that moment and she knew she'd feel the same contentment even if they were on a bench in Kent, as long as she was with Luciano.

'Think we could stay here for ever?' he asked, his eyes closed as he lifted his face to the sun.

'It's very tempting.'

Unfortunately, their peace didn't last long as they heard the roar of a supercar, a thud and screams of distress.

They both immediately began running in the direction of the heart-wrenching shrieks. Thoughts of themselves and their oasis of peace were forgotten in the face of someone else's tragedy.

The screech of tyres disappeared into the distance while the crowd congregated around someone lying in the middle of the road, and that told them everything about what had happened.

'Let me through, please. I'm a doctor.' Luciano took charge of the scene, making his way towards the casualty.

'They didn't stop. Just mowed him down.'

'I got the registration.'

'Is he going to be all right?'

The crowd, obviously in shock from what they'd witnessed, were all English tourists Sophie recognised from the ship. A few of the locals came rushing over, mobiles in hand as they phoned for help.

'What's his name?' Luciano was already on the ground, checking the elderly man's pulse.

'Charles.'

'Charles, can you hear me? I'm a doctor. You've been hit by a car. I'm just going to check you over. If you can, let me know where it hurts.' The only response was a series of groans.

'He hit his head hard on the ground when he landed. It sort of bounced.' One of his companions was able to give them enough information to understand there could be a serious head injury involved.

Sophie let Luciano carry on with his assessment whilst she dealt with the man's leg, which had clearly suffered some trauma. His trousers were ripped and although there wasn't any blood visible, the lower right leg was bruised and swollen. The ankle was bent at an odd angle too.

'Does anyone have any blankets or towels? Give me your shoelaces or belts. Anything I can use here.' She was sure the beachgoers would have something she could commandeer to support his leg.

Luciano flicked a glance at her. 'Is everything all right, Sophie?'

She gathered the donated beach towels, using them to pad the affected area, and tied them securely in place with the belts at her disposal, keeping Charles's leg as straight as possible. 'Suspected fracture of the fibula. I've got it.'

The bone hadn't pierced the skin so there was less risk of infection setting in but it would require X-rays to confirm the location and severity of the break.

He nodded and got back to treating the head injury. In the short time they'd known each other they'd worked together sufficiently to trust each other to make the right decisions and it warmed her heart to think of it.

* * *

Luciano was glad Sophie was here to help treat the casualty. They made a good team. He didn't have to worry about anything other than treating whatever head injury had been sustained when she was so capable of managing everything else. A high-velocity crash could cause multiple injuries, internal and external. Bones could mend given time but a brain injury could have a life-changing impact.

'Charles, I need to give you an examination to see where you've been hurt.' He was still breathing but he was falling in and out of consciousness. The velocity of the impact would have jarred his brain against his skull but without scans or X-rays there was no way of knowing how much damage had been done.

'There's blood coming from his nose and ears. It's possible he's suffered a skull base fracture. He's got a few lacerations on his scalp but no sign of skull depression.' He kept Sophie up to date with his assessment as she had with the lower limbs. With no apparent palpable dent in the skull he hoped that meant there were no pieces of skull embedded in the brain, which would require surgery to be removed. All they could do was immobilise him until help arrived and prevent any secondary injuries occurring that could arise from moving him carelessly.

'Take a few of these towels to stabilise his neck.' She tossed him a couple of towels, which he folded in half and then rolled up into colourful burrito shapes and placed either side of Charles's head.

'I need to go.' Charles began to come around but was disoriented and kept trying to sit up.

'You need to stay where you are until the ambulance comes.' Luciano pushed firmly on his shoulders, careful not to jolt his neck but determined not to let him sit up.

'I don't need an ambulance. What's going on?' It wasn't unusual for a patient to become confused in these circumstances but it was Luciano's job to keep him still until treatment could be administered.

'You've been in an accident, Charles. I think you might have a broken leg and you've hit your head. We need you to stay still.' Sophie tried her best to reassure him whilst also keeping his leg straight to prevent any further injury.

He kicked out with his other leg, knocking Sophie onto the ground. Although aggression was sometimes part of the job when patients were agitated by their condition, Luciano immediately came to Sophie's defence.

'Hey! You can't lash out like that. I know you're confused and in pain but we're trying to help you. Sophie, are you okay?' If he wasn't so intent on keeping this man stabilised until help arrived, he would've swept Sophie up in his arms and carried her away to safety. The thought of anyone hurting her brought out the protective streak in him he'd thought he'd never have to deal with again. He knew it meant he was in too deep already. Now that he cared so much about her, and her safety, it left him open to getting hurt again too.

'He knocked me off balance, that's all.' She gave him that 'Don't fuss' glare that made him smile.

'If you want to go, I can handle this.' He couldn't bear her to take any more abuse for simply providing assistance.

'I'm okay. You're just a bit confused about what's happening, Charles, aren't you?' Sophie didn't appear to bear the patient any ill will over the incident, which only elevated her in Luciano's esteem.

Thankfully the sound of sirens could be heard not far in the distance. Once the paramedics arrived they could take over and give

Charles the best treatment available. Then he and Sophie would be free to enjoy what they had left of their day together.

'Is there anything you'd like to do here before we go back? You didn't really get a chance to see the place.' Once Luciano had passed on the information about Charles's possible brain injury and leg fracture to the paramedics, there was the small matter of contacting the ship to let them know what had happened.

Sophie was left to watch from the sidelines, coming down from the rush of helping to treat their patient at the scene. She had neither the language skills nor contacts to help with the follow-up and was content to let Luciano deal with it. He was good at being in charge—level-headed in a crisis. Yet there was that other spontaneous side of him, which she was sure not many people got to see, the impulsive romantic who would take over a whole kitchen to impress her with his cooking skills. She could do with more of that in her life, given the chance. For now, she had to make do with whatever time they had left together.

'I don't want to go too far. I'm exhausted. How about a walk along the beach? It looks beautiful.' They'd come here to relax and after the drama she could use a little calm as long as she had Luciano to share it with her.

'I think we can manage that.' Luciano helped her down the large step from the promenade onto the shore. The first thing she did was remove her sandals so she could feel the sand beneath her feet. It was so soft she began to sink into it.

'We'll have to start moving before I disappear into this quicksand.' She began walking while Luciano went barefoot too. When he caught up with her at the water's edge she was pleased to see he'd rolled up his sleeves and loosened the top buttons of his shirt, looking more relaxed and off duty now.

'I think you're a real water baby, Sophie. Always drawn to the sea,' he said as she splashed through the soft waves slipping silently onto the beach.

'I find it soothing. The steady rhythm of the waves is like a lullaby to me. It helps me destress.' It was something she'd learned about herself on this trip. Perhaps she should move closer to the coast or buy herself a houseboat when she got back to bring more contentment to her life.

'Destressing is something we both need and I have just the place to do it. Come.' He laced his fingers through hers and lifted her hand to his mouth to kiss it. She didn't care where he was taking her because right now she would follow him to the ends of the earth if he asked her to. This was the perfect holiday romance—if she disregarded the work element and those life-or-death dramas.

To the right they had the beautiful seascape of the Mediterranean glittering in the sun. To the left they passed a strip of luxurious hotels, where she could picture movie stars swarming during film awards season. One even had the red carpet laid out for its exclusive guests. It was fabulous and a long way from her semi-detached in Kent. When Luciano rerouted them off the beach and towards one of the lavish entrances she suddenly felt out of her depth.

'We can't go in there.' She brushed the sand off her feet and shook out her sandals before putting them back on.

'Why not?' He didn't seem at all fazed by the notion of being part of the scene.

'It's a place for movie stars and rich people. They'll take one look at me and send for Security in case I taint the place with my working-class DNA.' Imposter syndrome set in as they got closer to the grand marble staircase leading to the hotel entrance. She was happy where they were and didn't need anyone looking down their nose at her and spoiling the daydream.

'Nonsense. You're beautiful and just as good as anyone else in there. The place can only be improved by having you there.' Luciano had such a confident charm it was easy to believe they could simply stroll in and that's exactly what they did.

She did, however, remain hovering in the doorway while he strode up to Reception so she could make a quick getaway if necessary. He chatted to the concierge at the desk—probably fluently in French to impress the slick fifty-something gatekeeper. He looked the sort who'd be impressed by the chief physician of a ship. Well, who wasn't?

The concierge summoned another junior member of staff, who was soon scurrying off to carry out whatever instructions had been issued. Luciano turned around and beckoned her over.

'Sophie, what are you doing all the way over there?' She took that as a cue they weren't about to be chased out of the building by security dogs chomping at their heels, trained to sniff out the riff-raff.

'Hey.' She slid her arm around his waist

and laid her head on his shoulder as though
it was the only way she could convince him
they were a couple. It only served to have
Luciano looking at her as though she'd gone
mad but he did drop a kiss on the top of her
head.

'*Merci pour votre aide,*' he said to his new
friend, and helped himself to the champagne
bucket and two glasses presented to him on
a silver tray.

'That's for us?' she asked as they followed
the junior member of staff through the hotel.

'*Oui. Pour toi, mon amour.*'

'If you're showing off your linguistic skills
to impress me, it's working.' Every language
he spoke only increased the exotic, erotic
nature of the man in her eyes. She couldn't
believe her luck that she'd met someone so
cultured who was interested in an English
Plain Jane like her. She had nothing to offer
except her nursing experience and sparkling
personality. Thankfully he seemed to have a
penchant for mouthy English girls.

'You haven't seen anything yet, *bella
donna*,' he whispered seductively into her
ear, turning her spine to gelato.

Any thoughts he'd conjured up in her
mind of holing up in a luxurious hotel suite
for an afternoon of passion vanished as they

exited the lobby and continued past the hotel swimming pool.

'Where are we going?' Now they'd left the bar and restaurant behind, she had no idea of their final destination.

Luciano thanked their attendant and slipped a discreet tip into the palm of his hand.

'That's us at the end of the pontoon.' He pointed down the walkway stretching out into the middle of the sea. It reminded her of one of the old-fashioned seaside piers except instead of amusement rides and carnival stalls this one housed several Bedouin-like tents.

They kept walking until they reached the end of the jetty, where the biggest structure sat on its own.

'Seriously? They're letting us use this?'

'Yes. I've paid for it. Sophie, you're as entitled as anyone else to be here. I know your confidence has taken a knock recently but you're a good person who works hard. You deserve a treat now and then.'

She didn't even know what the treat was supposed to be. From this angle it appeared to be a four-poster bed with three sides encased in a calico material, the front drapes left open and tied to the sides with purple silk rope. The bed, or sun lounger, she wasn't sure which it was, was festooned with satin cushions in opulent deep purples and mulberry colours.

'It's a daybed,' Luciano told her, as if that explained everything. 'I told them we wanted our privacy so no one will bother us.'

'This is amazing. Look at the view.' Standing on the edge of the pontoon, she could see the whole promenade in the distance and the cruise ship farther out to sea.

Luciano adopted his casual look again, removing his shoes and rolling his trouser legs up to his knees before sitting on the edge of the decking. He patted the space next to him for Sophie and she joined him once she was barefoot again too. Dipping her toes into the water was bliss—not as cold as she'd imagined but cool enough to counter the heat of the afternoon sun.

He poured two glasses of champagne and that first hit of bubbles on Sophie's tongue almost did as good a job as Luciano at making her feel fabulous. She leaned back on her elbows, splashing her feet in the water and drinking in the laid-back atmosphere.

'You know, we'd be more comfortable in the bed I hired for the day.'

'Uh-huh? Whose benefit would that be

for, mine or yours?' She flicked her foot and splashed water over him to cool his ardour.

'There's no reason why it couldn't be mutually beneficial.' He leaned over and kissed her. It was a long, languid affair that liquefied her bones and organs alike, leaving her a puddle of hormones at his touch.

Eyes closed and revelling in the taste of him, she felt his arm slipping under her knees and a floating sensation as he scooped her up and carried her over to the bed.

'We can't… Not here.' She was breathless from the romance of the setting but she hadn't completely lost her mind.

'No one can see us, Sophie. I want to make love to you.' There was nothing she wanted more, her body throbbing with need for him. It was just the matter of her unwillingness to become an exhibitionist that prevented her from fully giving in to temptation.

He dotted kisses around her neck as he joined her on the soft bed, doing nothing to help her resist. When he slid the straps of her sundress down and exposed more of her skin to his attentions she knew the last vestiges of her willpower would disappear with the rest of her clothes.

'Luciano…' She had to swallow her breathy

plea, her mouth as dry as the rest of her was wet.

'Okay. I don't want you to feel inhibited in any way.' Luciano moved away, taking his silky mouth and strong hands with him. For one horrible second Sophie thought he was calling it a day, his spontaneously sexy adventure brought to an abrupt end because she couldn't fully relax.

Instead, he discreetly pulled the drapes closed, leaving them totally obscured from outside view. Apart from the sound of the waves lapping against the pontoon, it was easy to believe they were ensconced in a completely private, luxurious hotel room.

'Happy now?' he asked as he undid his shirt.

Sophie sat up for a better view. 'I will be after the strip show.'

Luciano complied with a sexy smirk and a wiggle of his hips as he unbuttoned his shirt. He gave her a quick flash of his gorgeous chest before covering up again.

'Boo. Get 'em off!' she heckled until her sexy stripper had divested himself of his shirt and tossed it at her, quickly followed by his trousers.

It was so much fun being with him. When

he wasn't weighed down with grief and guilt, he was the sort of man she could picture herself being with. There would never be a dull moment when he was constantly surprising her and trying to make her happy. She was a lucky woman and she wished she could hold onto this feeling, this man, for ever.

The thought struck her hard as he bounded onto the bed with that glint in his eye that made her shriek with sheer delight. He would never expect her to change who she was to suit his expectations. He'd known who she was from the first time she'd challenged him in that treatment room. They'd shared their fears and had entered into this fling knowing what scars they both bore from the past.

For now, she had nothing to lose by indulging in this holiday fantasy and everything to gain in confidence and gorgeous memories. Luciano was providing her with a particularly yummy one now, stripping away her clothes to cover her naked body with his. What could be more exciting than making love outdoors and feeling as though they were the only two people in the world?

'Don't hold back,' she gasped, desperate for his body to join hers and make some more of those memorable moments he'd been so generous with so far.

'Are you sure?' His voice was strained with the restraint he was unnecessarily clinging to on her behalf.

'Love me, Luciano.' She hadn't meant to say those words but it was what she was thinking. For one afternoon she wanted to believe she was the most important person in his world because he was the most important person in hers.

She opened to him, body and soul, and Luciano took possession of everything she offered with a powerful thrust. With him inside her she was complete, whole again, and back to the woman she had been before domesticity and a cheating ex had snuffed out her spark. Luciano had brought her back to herself.

They rocked together, their bodies wrapped tightly around one another, the sheen of sweat glistening on their naked skin. When she reached that peak of total ecstasy she forgot where they were, letting anyone nearby know how much her lover was satisfying her. Luciano echoed her cries soon after.

They collapsed giggling together at their outdoor exploits. Sophie didn't know how she was going to show her face back in the hotel.

If the residents and staff hadn't heard exactly what they'd been up to she was sure the great big smile on her face would tell them.

Luciano couldn't remember the last time he'd felt so happy and content. They were hidden away from the rest of the world and experiencing that post-sex euphoria that made everything seem possible. He knew this wasn't real, yet he wanted it all. He wanted Sophie, the walks along the beach, the talking and laughing and making love to last for ever.

He'd never thought he'd feel this way again about anyone but he wanted to be with her all the time. Not in an unhealthy, stifling, toxic relationship but in that loving, couldn't-imagine-being-without-her way. They'd gone into this thinking it couldn't be any more than a fling and they'd go their separate ways when Sophie left to return home. However, with all the signs indicating they were both getting over their past traumas and finding something in each other that made them want to move on, he was reluctant to accept this could be over.

They hadn't discussed anything beyond her trip and he didn't know if being together was even feasible but he knew he wanted to try. He wanted to find a way to keep her in his life. If she didn't yet feel the same way about him then he needed to give her a reason to stay until she did.

CHAPTER TEN

PALMA, ON THE island of Mallorca, was their last port of call before Barcelona, where Sophie would be disembarking for the final time before flying back to England. What made the occasion sadder was that she couldn't spend her last day with Luciano because he was working.

Her trip was no longer about exploring new places, as lovely as they were, but about spending time with him. It was him that was bringing out the old Sophie, not the surroundings. When she was with him there was excitement, adventure and all those other things she'd been craving.

Perhaps she could be really impulsive and join him on the ship. After all, she'd already been approved as part of the crew. That way she wouldn't be making a long-term commitment simply to him. It would give them a chance to be together whilst continuing to have some fun and adventure with the pressure off their relationship. The only problem was that she'd have to return home to sort things out. But it would be worth it to extend this adventure.

The idea was impetuous and risky…and it was very *Sophie*, the old Sophie before she'd compromised herself in the name of love.

She put the idea on the back burner while she did some sightseeing. There were some beautiful cathedrals but it didn't seem right to visit them without Luciano. Instead, she did the typical tourist thing and went shopping. The narrow streets housed dozens of traditional Spanish shops perfect for browsing and marvelling at the local handicrafts. There was also a range of designer retailers occupying some of the most architecturally stunning premises. She only dared window shop in those.

When she'd finished exploring the town, she made her way back towards the marina. She needed coffee to fuel her for the rest of the day and the best place to do that was somewhere with a good view. Carefully choosing a spot that was good for people-watching as well as appreciating the beauty of the city, she took a seat outside and ordered from the nearest waitress.

'*Café con leche, por favor.*' It wasn't much but it was an attempt to ingratiate herself with the locals. Her efforts didn't go unrewarded as her coffee arrived with a complimentary pastry covered with powdered sugar.

'*Muchas gracias.*'

'Is this seat taken?'

She had to tilt her head back to see the face of the man wanting to share her personal space, although her pitter-pattering heart told her exactly who it was attempting to chat her up.

'It is now.' She patted the seat next to her.

Luciano kissed her on the cheek before sitting down. 'I see you're treating yourself. Sorry I wasn't here to do it for you.'

'I think you more than made up for that last night.' She lowered her sunglasses to give him what she hoped was a sultry look. At the mere mention of their night-time shenanigans, arousal was hitting all the same spots Luciano had helped her rediscover. With any luck they'd get a chance to do it all over again tonight.

Her seduction attempt was interrupted by their returning waitress and she was forced to change the subject. 'What are you doing here anyway? I thought you were supposed to be working. It's not a complaint, trust me. It's made my day, seeing you here.'

'You certainly know how to stroke a man's ego. I'm actually on an extended lunch break. I came down hoping to see you.'

'Oh, yeah? I was thinking about you too.' She was strangely touched by the fact that she'd been on his mind. If she was prepared to make some big life changes to join him on his travels, it was reassuring to know she'd be welcome. In his bed, or her bed, she wasn't fussy.

She bounced on the well-upholstered sofa as if to test its durability. 'If you can't wait until tonight, I think this should hold up to the job. But only if you don't mind having an audience.'

It was a ludicrous proposition, with the amount of tourists milling about, but she wanted to keep things light. She didn't want him to think any future plans were based entirely around him. Change had been needed for a long time and her time away had provided the catalyst. There was no way she was giving everything up just for a man again, even if it wouldn't be as much of a sacrifice second time around.

Her antics had the desired effect as the usually smooth Luciano almost snorted coffee up his nose with surprise. He wiped away the drops that had spilled down his shirt with a smirk. 'That's...er...a tempting offer but I'd prefer a little more privacy, thanks. We're in no rush, are we? We've got all night.'

The prospect of that was making her thirstier by the second.

'I've actually been thinking about making it more than just tonight.' She drank her coffee, hoping the caffeine in her system would give her the extra boost she needed to have this conversation.

Luciano's eyes were as wide as saucers and for a moment she thought she'd misread their set-up. It was casual, a fling, but suggesting they extend it beyond this holiday wasn't what they'd agreed.

'I mean, only if you wanted to.'

He grabbed her hand. 'Yes. Sorry. That's sort of what I wanted to talk about. Why I wanted to see you. This doesn't have to be over. I realised we...er...haven't been using any protection. I know it might be too late to ask now but I wondered if you were on any contraceptive?'

Sophie shook her head. Yes, they'd been stupid not to consider the consequences of what they'd been doing. Caught up in the romance and passion, she'd forgotten the reality and possible repercussions of their carelessness. Neither of them was naive and they should've known better, taken precautions. It had been so long since either of them had had casual sex they'd simply got carried away. Unfortunately, hindsight or making excuses wasn't going to change what they'd done. They'd had fun pretending they were invincible but playing with fire could lead to her getting burned. That was the one thing she was trying to avoid.

'You could take the morning-after pill but I wanted you to know that if it came to it, I wouldn't mind at all.'

'What do you mean?'

This wasn't the conversation she'd expected to have. Some flirting, maybe a nod towards their future together but nothing serious. How could she have been so stupid? A pregnancy now would ruin any future plans she had for travelling, snuffing out that last hope she had of ever breaking free from the prison Ryan had created for her.

'I'd like to be a father someday so if you were pregnant I wanted you to know I'd stand by you. It might not be the most conventional start to a relationship but this could be my second chance at a family. A reason for us to stay together.' Luciano was sitting on the edge of the seat as though the prospect of an unplanned pregnancy was something to celebrate.

'Luciano, it's very early days for us to be thinking about that sort of thing. I can't hang about here waiting to find out if I'm pregnant just to ease your conscience. You might want to have a family, but that's not reason enough for me to stay. Besides, I've told you, I want to do some travelling.'

Fear was bubbling up inside her with every hopeful word he uttered. He wanted her to be pregnant so he could be a father, with no consideration of how she'd feel about it. There was no mention of him wanting to be with her because it felt right. Because he loved her. It was the sign of another self-centred man who'd never put her first.

'Only yesterday I was thinking to myself that I'd like to go home and see my family. You could come too. I could set up my own practice out there. You wouldn't have to do anything but rest up and keep our baby safe.'

His excitement would be laughable if it wasn't for the fact that he was mapping out her future for her and taking it to an even more serious level than she could ever have predicted. They'd had a couple of nights together and he was already picking out baby names. Worse than that, he had her bubble-wrapped and securely locked up so nothing happened to their imaginary baby. It was a far cry from the exotic cruise doctor exploring the world who represented no threat to her freedom and far too close to a jailer for her to be comfortable.

Alarm bells were ringing so loudly in her ears they were giving her a headache. This was her worst nightmare come true. She wasn't going to trade a life of domesticity in England for the same in Italy and end up back where she'd started. Meeting his parents would've been a big enough deal for her at present and not in keeping with her idea of adventure, never mind actually setting up home together as well.

She withdrew her hand and sat back, creating some distance and perspective. 'Luciano, I'm sure there are a lot of women who'd love that idea but I haven't planned that far ahead. I'm very much in the moment these days.'

'*Sì*. I know we've only just met but that's exactly why you're the reason I'm seeing everything so differently now. That's why I think we should be mad and really go for it.'

'What are you talking about?' Her spontaneity had apparently rubbed off on him in the most bizarre fashion.

'Marry me, Sophie.'

'What? No. Stop being ridiculous.' She was on her feet, her blood turning to ice at the horror that was unfolding. A proposal of marriage after a few days together was the opposite of what she wanted. He clearly didn't know her at all. But why should he when this wasn't supposed to have been anything more than a holiday hook-up?

'Hear me out. We're good together, yes? You want to move somewhere new. You can come to Italy with me and we could start a family. Even if you're not pregnant now, it's something we could work on. Losing Renata showed me that life is too short to let the good things slip away. You're the best thing to happen to me in a long time, Sophie.'

'That's not a good reason for me to give up my life and all my future plans.' That fear was closing in around her, suffocating the life out of her the way her last relationship had. Only this time she could end up pregnant and alone in a different country when he decided she wasn't what he wanted after all.

'You said yourself you wanted more and you're the only person I know I'd ever consider marrying again.' She believed he meant what he was saying at that moment but that didn't constitute a good motive for her. He needed a replacement for his wife so he could go back to his old life without too much disruption. That wasn't going to be her.

The reason she'd fallen for Luciano was because of the person he was now, here, with the life she was envious of, not one she'd dread.

'I meant as a work colleague, a travelling companion, good company, an excellent lover. Not a husband. Not someone I'm tied to for the rest of my days. I'm sorry, Luciano, we should call this what it is—a holiday romance. That's it. Tomorrow I'm going home and we'll leave things as they are now. Goodbye.'

She was shaking as she walked away, gulping back the sob bubbling up from deep inside. Ending things wasn't what she wanted but she couldn't see an alternative. Committing herself for the rest of her life to someone she hardly knew would be a sign of desperation on both their parts, an even bigger trap than buying a house with someone. Especially if she moved what would feel like halfway across the world to somewhere she didn't even know the language, never mind anybody or anything else.

'Why did you have to ruin things, Luciano?' she cried out, much to the surprise of the other passengers she passed on her way back to the ship.

Instead of going home tomorrow excited and full of plans, she would be returning with a heart heavier than ever. She'd fallen for the wrong man again but this time she wasn't going to wait until everything fell apart around her.

Somehow the timing didn't make a difference. Her heart had taken another hammering, irrespective of her new so-called attitude or preventative measures. Love had a whole lot to answer for when it was capable of destroying a person's world once the rose-tinted glasses came off.

Luciano wanted to run after Sophie but she obviously needed space away from him. He paid the bill and walked back towards the ship a lot less enthused than when he'd left. He'd read the situation completely wrong. Thinking she'd appreciate the spontaneity of his proposal, he'd launched into it without proper consideration, carried away by the notion of starting a family with her back home. He'd thought he'd never want to put himself through the heartache again but beginning to imagine it with Sophie had proved he wanted it as much as ever. The idea of having Sophie in his life, along with the chance to become a father, had felt like hitting the jackpot in the casino.

If he'd taken the time to recount the conversation they'd had, the way she'd shrunk away from him at the suggestion of having a baby together, he would've realised he was pushing her too quickly. Instead he'd panicked and thrown the biggest commitment he could at her in the hope she'd realise he was serious—that he was moving on from Renata. He could see now that his actions seemed desperate rather than impulsive, but it didn't have to mean the end for them.

Running out of time to make amends, he gave chase, catching up with her just before she boarded the ship.

'Sophie! Wait!' He saw her hesitation before she stopped, which broke his heart a little more. She'd briefly considered carrying on and pretending not to hear him, without giving him one last chance.

'We can't leave it like this, Sophie. Forget what I said. It was a spur-of-the-moment, idiotic thing to say.'

'Which part? Having a baby with someone I hardly know? Getting married? Giving up everything so you can lock me away until I produce the next in the Montavano line? I can't just forget it, Luciano. I don't want any of that and I won't marry you, now or ever.' She left no room for misunderstanding with the brutal rejection.

'Okay, okay, I'm sorry. Marriage is off the table but we can still be together. You said you wanted to travel. You could still come out here. We could find a way to make this work.'

As she shook her head she dislodged the tears clinging to her eyelashes. It wasn't a good portent for future plans.

'I don't think so. Not now. You've reminded me how very different we are.'

'Opposites attract,' he said in a last-ditch attempt to convince her.

'No one's doubting there's chemistry between us but I think we're incompatible where it matters. I've been in that kind of relationship before. It doesn't work unless we compromise who we are for the other person. I'm not prepared to do that again for anyone.'

'Tell me what you want me to do to make

this right. I'll do whatever it takes to salvage this.'

'Don't you see? Then you're compromising who you are and what you want in order to keep me happy. It's not a recipe for success. It's not being honest. I was attracted to you because I thought it was exciting giving everything up to sail around the world. It's become clear that's not the real you. You ran away from the life you had but deep down you need to admit to yourself it's the one you want back. There's nothing wrong with that but I can't be part of it. If I give up my job and my home it will be to do something amazing, something exciting. I'm afraid settling down again isn't part of that.'

'You don't think what we've shared hasn't been amazing and exciting?'

'You know it was but unless we spend the rest of our days on board this ship, it simply isn't sustainable. I don't want what you're offering. You need a partner who's going to stick around long term and give you babies. I'm not that girl. Thank you for everything, Luciano. I'm never ever going to forget you, or this trip, but it's over.' She swiped her tears away and forced a smile that made him want to weep too.

'So this is really goodbye?' He couldn't

quite believe how this was ending when last night their future had seemed so full of possibilities. This morning when he'd remembered they hadn't used any contraception he'd had that same frisson in his veins, his blood pumping harder around his body, as if she'd shown him a positive pregnancy test. There was a chance of a baby, of becoming a father, having a family again, and that prospect had overridden all the pain that had caused in the past. Even if he couldn't have all that, he still wanted Sophie in his life.

'Yes.' Her tone and body language were firm, but it was Sophie who instigated one last sad, lingering kiss. It only reinforced the enormity of his loss to have her walk out of his life. Grief attacked his body like a swarm of bees stinging him all over, piercing his skin and poisoning his blood until his throat swelled up and he couldn't breathe.

'Goodbye, Luciano. I'll never forget you.'

He was so choked up, so desolate as she left him standing there that he didn't even get to say a last farewell before she was gone.

Though they hadn't known each other long, he knew life was never going to be the same without her. She'd shown him that

trast between ...
offered her away from he...
It had been too much, too soon. If he a...
given her time to get used to sharing her life with someone again, they might have had a different outcome. She would never have married him but she might have been

he couldn't hide for ever. He had a family and a life to return to. He only wished Sophie was going back to it with him.

...o tears. 'I am so happy

'So I see. Now, are you going to invite me in or let me freeze out here on your doorstep?'

'Sorry. Come in.' Sophie stood aside to let her neighbour shuffle inside. She was still

CHAPTER ELEVEN

IT HAD BEEN five weeks since Sophie had returned home. In some ways it seemed more like five years. Sometimes more like five hours. She'd gone straight back to work as though she'd never left, which hadn't helped her sullen mood.

It was nice to see her patients and colleagues but nothing here was as thrilling as anything she'd left back at the ship: sun, sea and sex with Luciano in exchange for senior citizens and bedpans. It wasn't in her nature to be mean but that was how it felt.

When Edith turned up at her door, unexpectedly, she burst int̶o̶ ̶t̶e̶a̶r̶s̶
to see you.'

trying to get used to the dramatic change in temperature herself, along with everything else. Never mind having to get up in the dark to go to work and cook her own meals, getting used to her own company again was leaving a lot to be desired in the wake of her holiday.

Edith flopped down onto her settee with a soft 'Oof.'

'You look well.' Sophie saw the colour in her cheeks and the renewed spark about her, probably as a result of being in the bosom of her family again. She knew how it was to thrive in the company of others.

When she'd been with Luciano she'd flourished. She'd actually felt herself blooming like a flower in the sun. Since coming home she'd withered, wilting into the shadows, and not merely because of the inclement weather. Part of her was missing. Her heart. She'd left it back on the ship with Luciano. Coming back had highlighted the con-working somewhere more glamorous, living somewhere gorgeous, loving someone fabulous. She might have been happy. At this moment in time she couldn't see how she could be any more miserable than she was now. If things hadn't worked out she could've moved on the way she used to do. A relationship didn't have to be a death sentence to the individual but she'd learned that too late.

'Mmm… I wish I could say the same about you. You look a bit under the weather, not at all how I left you on the ship. Missing your doctor?'

Sophie wasn't sure if it was Edith's on-point perception or her knowing wink that unnerved her more. She'd always been able to see right through her. All the times she'd thought she'd adequately faked her happiness with Ryan, Edith had known all along what had been going on.

'No. Not at all,' she spluttered, her denial too quick to be plausible. 'I have been a bit peaky. It might be a stomach bug or something.'

Sophie could feel Edith's eyes burning into her soul, seeing the lie for herself, but it wasn't going to make any difference to her situation by telling her the truth. She'd only worry or blame herself for the predicament Sophie currently found herself in.

'Maybe you need a holiday.' Edith's mischievous, twinkly-eyed smile managed to stop her from feeling sorry for herself for a moment.

'Ha-ha.' That was what had got her into this mess in the first place. 'I don't think I'll be travelling again any time soon.'

'That's a shame. I was half expecting you to have eloped with Dr M. by the time I got back.'

She had nothing to say to that.

'There was a definite spark between you two and then he went to all that trouble so I could speak to you.'

There seemed little point in holding back the truth when Edith had it all figured out anyway. 'We might have had a bit of a fling.'

Sophie tried to fake nonchalance but even the mention of it made her blush, her heart pumping all the harder.

'I knew it!' Edith clapped her hands together, clearly delighted by the news. 'I'm so pleased for you.'

Sophie held out a hand before she got so carried away by the idea of their romance that she bounced off the settee and did herself an injury. 'It was a fling, that's all. We haven't stayed in touch but it's not all bad news. That trip made me realise how unhappy I am with my lot. I've handed in my notice at work and I'm thinking of selling up. No idea what I'm doing after that but I have to make a change.'

'Good.'

It wasn't the reaction she'd expected, especially when it had taken Sophie considerably longer to come to the conclusion it would be the best course of action for her.

'I know it must come as a shock to you. You've been such a good neighbour and friend, Edith. I can never thank you enough for the cruise and I'll come and visit you when I can.' Edith was the one thing she'd worried about when making her decision. She'd had so many health problems and with her family living abroad she didn't have anyone else looking out for her.

'Don't you worry about me. I'm glad to see you getting your spark back. Actually, I have some news for you too. That's why I came back. John wants me to go and live with him and the family in Spain. He's gone now to see the estate agent about putting the house up for sale. I said yes, of course. I'm getting on a bit and I don't want to miss whatever time I have left with my family.'

'That's fantastic. I'm so pleased for you.' Sophie went over to give her a hug, tears forming with happiness that Edith wasn't going to be alone any more, but also with sadness at losing her friend.

'You'll come and visit me. John says there's a bed for you whenever you need one. I've told everyone how you've looked after me and I know they're looking forward to meeting you. You will stop by on your travels, won't you?' There was a slight waver in Edith's bravado that almost set Sophie off too. She was worried they might never see each other again and the thought was too horrible to contemplate.

'It will be top of my list of places to visit,' she reassured Edith. Since going to recuperate with her family, she had a new lease of life. Instead of sitting in her front room by the gas fire, watching daytime TV, Sophie could see herself dining al fresco under the Spanish sun.

It brought unbidden images of Luciano, sitting around a table sharing antipasto with his family in the idyllic Italian countryside. Would that really have been so bad? Being part of that couldn't be worse than sitting here at night alone with a TV dinner on her knees.

Edith's fantastic recovery was proof that the power of love could work wonders for a person. At the time she couldn't believe Luciano could have fallen in love with her so quickly, that it was simply the euphoria of a new romance clouding his judgement. Yet deep down she knew he wouldn't have proposed unless he'd meant it when marriage and family had been so important to him. She'd had a lot of time to think since coming back and had come to the conclusion that it was the thought of falling in love with Luciano that had scared her more than anything. It left her feeling vulnerable and she had a right to be wary after the fallout from her last impulsive dive into a relationship. Except she reckoned she was suffering more being so far away from Luciano than if they'd attempted a long-term relationship and failed.

'Earth to Sophie.' Edith interrupted her wandering mind to remind her that they were both sitting in her living room and not lying on the deck of a cruise ship.

'Pardon?'

'Your thoughts are clearly still back there with your dishy doc. Is there no hope of you two getting back together?' The idea of a fling was probably an alien concept to Edith, who'd married her first love and been with him for forty-five years. There hadn't been anyone else. To her generation, when you met 'the one' you never let them go, even after death.

She thought of Luciano and his grief for his wife and unborn children. He'd had the same opinion when she'd first met him. That no one could replace the love he'd lost. By the end of the holiday he'd proposed to her. Perhaps she'd meant more to him than just a mere replacement for what he'd lost. She'd thrown it back in his face and run home. Away from temptation, away from a chance of loving again and away from being loved. Instead, she'd played it safe, or so she'd thought. Now she was alone and more broken-hearted than ever.

She shook her head. 'I said some horrible things I can never take back. I wouldn't even know where to find him.'

'You've thought about it?'

She'd thought of little else over these past weeks and how different her life could have been. They could've found a way to make it work, or at least tried.

'He's crossed my mind on occasion,' she said with a wry smile she knew wouldn't fool Edith.

'I'm sure the cruise company could track him down for you. Trust me, the only things you regret are the things you didn't take a chance on.' Edith got to her feet and Sophie escorted her to the door with the warning ringing in her ears, reinforcing what her gut and her heart were already telling her to do. Take a chance.

'I'll think about it. In the meantime, you take care of yourself and let me know if there's anything I can do for you.'

'John's sorting everything out for me but I will want to see you before we go back. Hopefully with a plane ticket in your hand and Luciano's itinerary.'

'I'm not making any promises.' She had to admire her soon-to-be ex-neighbour's tenacity. It was that sheer bloody-mindedness that had no doubt saved her life on the holiday and now she was equally as determined to see Sophie and Luciano paired off. If only it was that simple.

Edith patted her on the cheek in that way only a grandmother could get away with. 'Don't live with any regrets.' She started off down the path then turned back. 'Oh, and tell him about the baby. It's only fair. He'd make a great dad.'

Sophie was left standing on the doorstep open-mouthed, wondering how on earth Edith had figured out the secret she'd been slowly coming to terms with herself. She'd come home with something more special than a fridge magnet to remind her of her trip. It was part of the reason she'd been prompted into making those big life changes, knowing that if she stayed as she was she'd be stuck in this rut for ever with a baby to raise. This was her last chance to get away, relocate and start over before she was tasked with the responsibility of raising another human—something that would require a certain level of stability.

She'd considered contacting Luciano. After everything he'd been through she knew how strong his desire was to have a family but confirming her pregnancy would have left her open to further complications. Luciano was currently under no obligation to her for anything, but a child would change that.

He would definitely want to be an integral part of their baby's life and she didn't know how that was going to work out if he was still sailing around the world. That's if he still wanted anything to do with her. They'd been caught in a romantic fantasy and the reality could prove different. He might've even found someone else by now. After all she'd told him, she didn't want anything he was offering. It wasn't true. She'd been scared of what he'd offered. A future. A family. For ever.

She wasn't going to put him under any obligation to do anything in case he had moved on and made different plans. When she told him about the baby she'd make that clear. It would be difficult enough to see him again after her brutal rejection of his proposal, without going back to dump some more life-changing news upon him.

Was she hoping for more than an acknowledgement of impending parenthood? Yes. It was too bad she'd tossed it away so carelessly and now she was afraid it was too late. Even if she knew how to contact him. Which she didn't. She definitely didn't.

CHAPTER TWELVE

'LET ME AT least set the table, *Mamma*,' Luciano pleaded, trying to be useful in some capacity.

'No. Sit. Sit. You are the guest of honour today.' His mother pushed down on his shoulders, forcing him into his seat at the head of the tables shoved together on the porch.

'This is *Papà's* seat. I haven't done anything to deserve it.' He was embarrassed by the fuss, his parents and siblings treating him as though he was a celebrity.

'You came back to us, son. That means more than anything.' Unnervingly, his stoic father was welling up as he shook his hand.

Luciano was forced to sit and watch as his family swarmed around him, filling the tables with enough food to feed an army. He felt like a fraud. A conman who'd benefited from the generosity of vulnerable people under false pretences. He didn't deserve praise and he certainly didn't want to celebrate past, or present, failures. Left to himself, he would have slipped quietly back into his old life as though he'd never run away from it.

'I came home a month ago. You made a big enough fuss then.' The crying, the kissing and hugging when he'd shown up unannounced had convinced him he'd made the right decision, although he hadn't imagined the outpouring of gratitude and affection to extend this long. He just wanted to get back to normal. At least as normal as it got around here without Renata or Sophie.

He hadn't stopped thinking about her. Whatever she'd thought, it had been more than a fling to him. When she'd gone home, the heart had gone out of the cruise life for him. He'd stuck it out for a little while longer, irrationally hoping their tryst had resulted in a pregnancy and she'd have to get in touch with him again. Given the chance to do things over, he'd play things differently and not to come on so strong.

As time had gone on without any word from her, he'd become restless, eager to join the real world again. That was still thanks to Sophie and he'd have preferred to have done it with her by his side. However, that wasn't to be and he'd simply have to get over it the same way he'd had to get used to the idea of living without Renata. This time he'd accept the comfort and support of his family, even though they knew nothing of his most recent heartbreak.

'But this is the first time the whole family has all been together since then.'

'Any excuse for a celebration, eh?' If he believed this was nothing but a ruse for his parents to feed them all up he wouldn't feel so undeserving.

'Do you honestly think they'd let the return of the prodigal son pass without a party?' His youngest sister, Carlotta, nudged him with one hip whilst balancing a toddler on the other. She set a bowl of olives on the table in front of him. It was the kind of sibling teasing he'd grown up with and had missed during his all-too-serious year away.

'I suppose I am the favourite,' he teased back.

'*Were*. There are a lot of younger cuties vying for your crown now.' With that she dumped her chubby cherub accessory into Luciano's lap.

'He's changed so much. They all have. I'm so sorry I stayed away for so long.' He cuddled his nephew, who hardly knew him, and watched the offspring of his brothers and sisters playing in the garden. He didn't know if he was apologising to the baby, his sister or himself. He'd missed a lot.

In his failure to become a father he'd been jealous, bitter at times when his family seemed to reproduce at the drop of a hat. Then his grief had kept him away, a recluse unwilling to engage with anyone. Finally, he'd run away to sea for the better part of a year. The whole time he'd been absorbed in his failure to have a family he'd ignored the one he already had at home. Now that he was back he wasn't going to take any of them for granted. Fate had stolen away his chance to be a husband or parent but he could still be a good son, brother and uncle. He had a life to lead that included so many wonderful people.

'We're just glad you're back, bro, and more like your old self. At least now we can ask you to babysit without worrying that you're going to top yourself.' His brother Sylvestro, as tactful as ever, slapped him on the back.

'Sylvestro!' It was his mother's horrified gasp he heard above all the other noise of cutlery and plates hitting the floor. The eyes of his family were all on his brother, chastising him for his forthright comment.

'What? You know we're all thinking it.' His beefy older brother held his hands up, apparently surprised he'd offended anyone present, including Luciano.

'You could have worded it better.' Emilia, the eldest of his siblings, threw an olive at him, which bounced off Sylvestro's head without making much impact.

'Sylv's not known for his subtlety, though, is he?'

'Don't worry, I'm available for guilt-free babysitting any time.' He didn't want anyone to feel bad on his account. Especially when his brother was just being honest. It was only now he could see what he'd put his family through. They'd been walking on eggshells, worried about his state of mind, and he'd selfishly shut them out. Goodness knew what they'd thought when he'd gone off to sea. He'd kept contact to a minimum, only phoning sporadically to let them know he was in the land of the living.

'Well, we're all happy you're here, Luciano. *Salute!*' His father raised a glass of wine and the rest of the family joined him in the toast.

He barely managed to lift his glass in response, overwhelmed by the love directed towards him, including from the two-year-old who was now swinging from his neck in an over-enthusiastic hug. 'Glad to be home.'

Perhaps it was his absence that had made his heart grow fonder, or it could be due to Sophie's influence. She'd shown him the difference it made to have someone close again.

'Is that a car coming up the lane?' Everyone followed his father's gaze towards the taxi making its way towards the villa.

Luciano did a quick head count and though he'd lost track of his family for a while he was pretty sure they were all here now. They didn't get many visitors out this way, so the sight of a taxi had everyone straining their necks trying to catch the first glimpse of who was in the back of the car. Unfortunately, his view was impeded by the toddler currently climbing on his head. He did hear the car pull up and the door open as someone got out.

'Who is that?' His sister's whisper was accompanied by his little brother Galen's wolf whistle.

'Ciao, possiamo aiutarti?'

His mother rushed out first to see how they could help the interloper. More out of curiosity than any other reason, he imagined.

'I…um… I'm looking for Luciano.'

There was no denying the owner of that English voice, despite her uncertainty. It had been haunting him for months.

He stood up, peeled off his nephew and handed him back to his mother. His whole body was electrified by the thought of her being here but he needed to see her for himself.

'Sophie?' He could feel the eyes of his family on him filled with questions and astonishment. But his only concern was the woman standing in the driveway, looking as though she was about to duck back into the taxi and make a quick getaway. He wasn't going to let her go a second time.

'I'm sorry. I didn't realise… I should have called ahead.' She gestured to his gathered family and he realised she was carrying a suitcase in her hand.

'No problem. I'm just glad to see you. Surprised, but happy.' Before she changed her mind about being here, he jumped down off the porch, paid the taxi driver and took her case. She wasn't going anywhere until he found out what had brought her here in the first place. 'How did you find me?'

She gave him an uncertain smile before flicking a glance over at their audience.

'You're a hard man to track down. I managed to get hold of Patrice—she's still working for the cruise line. She told me you'd left and I remembered the name of the village you came from. It took a bit more trouble to get information about the family vineyard from the locals with my limited grasp of the language.'

She'd gone to a lot of trouble to find him. He wanted to believe she'd thought him worth it rather than being simply a stop on her grand tour.

'Are you staying for a while?'

'I, er, don't know. That depends on you. I didn't realise you were back living with your parents. I'm sure I can find a hotel nearby.'

'Not at all. My mother would never allow it. I'm here temporarily after selling my house until I find somewhere new.' There was so much he wanted to say, so much he needed to ask her, but it would have to wait until they had some privacy…which could prove difficult at a family dinner hosted in his honour.

'*Buona sera.*'

'A friend of my brother's?'

'Aren't you going to introduce us, Luciano?'

Sophie was inundated with greetings and

handshakes, Luciano with questioning looks. How did he even begin to explain this when he didn't know what had brought her here?

'Sophie, meet the family. Family, meet Sophie.' It was a meeting she'd told him not so long ago was too much, too soon and now here she was under her own steam.

He ushered her through the curious throng of family members to the front of the house, where she was ambushed by his father.

'Sit. Sit.' He set a place for her at the table whilst everyone scrambled to sit next to her as though she was some sort of sideshow. 'Galen, take the lady's bag to the spare room.'

'How did you two meet?' Carlotta, the romantic, could probably hear wedding bells already.

Luciano didn't want to embarrass Sophie, or his parents, with the truth of what had happened between them. Neither did he know if that was what had brought her out here or if it was mere curiosity when she'd once expressed interest in seeing his home.

She met his eyes across the table, begging him to help her out.

'We met on the ship. Sophie was a passenger, a nurse, who helped out during that rogue wave.' He had mentioned the incident in passing but nothing about falling for one of the passengers during the crisis.

His mother crossed herself and said a prayer. 'I'm so happy my son is on dry land but tell me, Sophie, what brings you out here, other than my son?' The interrogation to uncover the truth began, assisted by the offer to pour Sophie a glass of lip-loosening wine.

He saw her cheeks go pink as she put her hand across the glass. 'Not for me, thanks.'

'Sophie prefers more exotic drinks. I'm sorry we can't offer you anything blue or with a paper parrot.'

The in joke made them both smile at the memory of that afternoon but he was aware they both remained the centre of attention.

'I'm fine. I'll be quite happy with a glass of water.'

His brother returned minus Sophie's luggage.

'You can stay as long as you like, Sophie.'

'Thank you. That's very kind, Mr Montavano.'

'Sophie might prefer to share Luciano's room, Pop. It is the twenty-first century. I couldn't figure out what had caused the change in my brother when he came home. Now I know. You're punching above your weight, Luciano, but good luck to you.' It was Sylvestro's wife who chastised his tact-lessness this time with an elbow to the ribs.

For the first time since he'd returned, he was regretting selling his own house, simply for the privacy it would have afforded them now. He couldn't bear the hopeful looks in his parents' eyes when there was no guar-antee Sophie would stick around, especially if she was going to be confronted by a bar-rage of personal questions and insinuations by this mob.

He kicked his chair back and went to res-cue Sophie before they scared her off alto-gether. 'I think Sophie and I will go for a walk. I know she's keen to see some of the Italian countryside.' He extended his hand towards her and she seemed grateful to take it.

'Nice to meet you all,' she said graciously, before they walked off hand in hand towards the green fields where they'd have space to breathe. And to talk.

'I'm so sorry about that. If I'd known you were coming I'd have arranged somewhere quieter, minus an audience.'

'It was a spur-of-the-moment decision. I quit my job, sold up and this was the first place that came to mind.'

'You're finally doing the travelling you'd planned?' He'd been hoping it was more about coming to see him but she'd already made it clear there wasn't a future for them.

'I haven't decided anything really.' She began picking some of the wildflowers nearby, concentrating on the posy she was gathering and not on him.

It didn't make any sense to him why she'd pack up her life in England and head out here without any plan. Not when she'd been so against the idea of risking everything when he'd suggested it.

'How's Edith?'

'She's really well. Her son invited her to go and live with him in Seville, so she's moved on too.' That meant Sophie was on her own, although that didn't fully explain why she'd come here.

'Forgive me, *cara mia,* but why are you really here? You didn't want to see me again after I proposed. I admit that was rash but I apologised. I was afraid of losing you or never seeing you again.'

She stopped rummaging in the under-growth to look at him. 'Do you really mean that?'

He took her hands and turned her round to face him. 'Of course I do. I don't go around proposing to just anyone. I haven't stopped thinking about you, Sophie. If you're not in a hurry to leave I'd really like to spend more time with you.'

He'd do whatever it took to convince her he was serious. If she was giving him a second chance to be with her, he'd grab it with both hands.

'I'd like that too but…er…there's something I have to tell you first.' Her throat bobbed as she swallowed and he could see she was anxious about saying anything more. Whatever it was, he was sure they could get through it if it meant they could start over together.

'You can tell me anything. I'm not going anywhere.' He hoped he could say the same about her.

'I'm pregnant.' She blurted it out, watching for his reaction. Luciano was too stunned to say or do anything whilst he processed that information.

'Say something. Even if it's only to tell me I'm on my own and you don't want anything to do with me or the baby. I came all this way to tell you and I have so I should go.'

'You're pregnant with our baby.' He was really going to be a parent. With Sophie. He almost fell to his knees with gratitude but he didn't think that move would go any better the second time around.

'Yes. I, um, haven't been with anyone else.' She mistook his disbelief for something negative when, in fact, this meant everything to him.

'I didn't mean… I haven't either, just so you know. We weren't very careful.' One could say perhaps subconsciously the lack of contraception had been about his desire for a family but he knew it was more about his desire for Sophie. They'd both been carried away in the heat of the moment and the passion they hadn't been able to escape.

When Sophie didn't seem as thrilled by the consequences as he was, his elation began to subside. She'd made the first move in coming out here to see him, to tell him, something she wouldn't have done if she didn't want to maintain a connection or have him in her life in some capacity. Now it was down to him to convince her to stay.

Sophie had never really had any doubt Luciano would take the news graciously. He was a gentleman and he wanted to be a father. His hesitation had thrown her so much she was in danger of collapsing. The relief as he accepted equal responsibility for her predicament was overwhelming. As much as she'd told herself she could do this on her own, being here, seeing Luciano, she realised how much she didn't want to.

'Are you okay?' Luciano slipped an arm around her waist to help her stay upright.

'Yeah. A little faint.' It was all she could do not to bury her head in his chest and ask him for a hug.

'Sit down. I'll go back and get you some water once I know you're not going to pass out.' He eased her down onto the grass and sat beside her.

'It's okay. Everything has just been a bit much for me on my own.' Only now had she admitted to herself she was out of her depth alone, pregnant, with no home or job to fall back on. What she'd thought of as a great adventure when she'd started out here had seemed more of a mistake with every passing minute. She'd barely given herself time to think since landing, coming here instead of checking into a hotel.

'You're not on your own any more.' Luciano put his arm around her shoulders and Sophie watched her tears drip onto the grass, clinging to the blades like fresh morning dew and feeling just as cleansing, like the start of a new day full of possibilities she hadn't dared hope for until now.

Then she remembered they hadn't seen each other in weeks. Even then they'd only been together for a few days. She might have been thinking about him this entire time, imagining what could have been and regretting turning him down. That didn't mean they were going to pick up where they'd left off. It was only natural he'd want to be part of his baby's life but she didn't know where she'd fit in. If at all. It wouldn't do to lie to herself that this was something it wasn't.

She shrugged his arm off but lamented the loss as the weight of it lifted from her.

'I don't want you to think you have to take me on too. I'm sure we can work something out between us over child care, once I figure out what I'm going to do for a job or a house.' She was trying not to panic but she hadn't given proper thought to the practicalities of travelling with a baby. It would be completely different as a new mum compared to the young singleton she'd been the last time she'd done it.

He scowled at her. 'Why wouldn't you stay here with me? I told you I'm here for you. Both of you. I know I scared you off by proposing and planning out a life together but I was serious about wanting this to work, Sophie.'

'Are you?' She'd been afraid to believe it had been anything more than a knee-jerk reaction to their time together, or living with the consequences of it, but he'd felt the same.

'I think I fell for you the moment you shouted at me over Edith's treatment,' he said with a grin.

'Mmm, I think it took me a little longer. Perhaps when you threw me out of your clinic like a boss.' She didn't know when exactly it had happened but it had been on the cards since that first meeting.

'I've missed you.' Luciano leaned forward and leaned his forehead against hers.

'Me too.' All the recent uncertainty and worry melted away when Sophie's lips met his in a soft kiss. She wanted this but she'd been so afraid of letting it happen or, worse, discovering Luciano wasn't the man she'd thought; she'd been in denial. Now she could actually express how she felt, it was liberating.

'I know things have moved faster than either of us were prepared for but I want to give us a chance.' He laid his hand gently on her slightly rounded belly.

'That's why I came.' Being with the man

she'd fallen for, raising a family of her own was something she was willing to risk everything to get right.

'I don't want to pressure you into anything you're not ready for. Perhaps we could rent a place together and see how it goes. I'm working in the emergency department at the local hospital. Maybe you could get a job there too or we could set up a medical practice of our own. If things work out, who knows where it could lead?'

'You might propose again?'

'If you're lucky.'

'I have some money from the sale of the house that could keep us going for a while too.'

'That's sorted, then. We're moving in together.'

They'd discussed the practicalities of her moving to Italy and raising their baby but she wanted more.

'It's not very romantic, is it?'

'Last time I tried to be romantic you called me ridiculous and left the country.'

'True, but I've had plenty of time to think since then.'

'And if I told you I still wanted to spend the rest of my life with you?'

Sophie screwed up her nose. 'I'm a bit

wary of the whole insta-love thing. I think great sex clouds judgement on that score.'

'What if I said I think I *could* fall in love with you and *could* see us growing old together?'

'Better. I think I *could* fall in love with you too.' Who was she kidding? She knew she would. It was only a matter of time since she was halfway there already. Even then it was only her wounded heart preventing her from going all in.

He kissed her again, reigniting the passion she'd only experienced once in her life before. It seemed more intense this time as they expressed their feelings towards one another.

Moving all the way to Italy, pregnant, to be with a man she'd only known for a brief time might seem risky to some, but it was exactly the sort of thing the old Sophie would have done. And that made her so very happy.

EPILOGUE

One year later

'*SEI PROPRIA BELLA, CARA.*'

'I thought it was bad luck to see the bride before the wedding?' Sophie spun around as Luciano entered the room.

'Since when did we stick to the rules?' He closed the distance between them quickly, took her hand and spun her round to get a full look at her wedding dress. 'You look beautiful.'

'You don't look so bad yourself.' Her heart continued to do that pitter-patter thing every time he came into a room but he looked so handsome in his tuxedo it went into over-drive.

Even though they'd opted for a low-key ceremony in the grounds of his parents' villa, they'd gone for traditional wedding attire. She'd had fun wedding-dress shopping with his sisters in some of the classiest Italian boutiques they could find. In the end, she'd fallen in love with the simple ivory silk gown she was wearing now. It had Luciano's approval too as he pulled her close and nuzzled into the flowers in her hair.

'You know we could skip the ceremony and go straight to the honeymoon,' he whispered, doing that thing that buckled her knees, almost convincing her to lock the bedroom door on the rest of the world.

'As tempting as that sounds, I don't think our families would approve of us abandoning them. Apart from which, I thought we were honeymooning at home?' She'd been looking forward to a few days together without him having to go to work.

Despite all her worries, the time they'd spent together during her pregnancy had only served to strengthen their bond. More importantly, they'd gotten to know each other properly, their feelings growing as a result. They'd rented an apartment for a few months after Sophie had moved to Italy but with the impending birth of their baby and the growing certainty that they wanted to be together, they'd purchased their own little haven in the country.

With the arrival of baby Alessandro, she'd

thought she couldn't be happier, until Luciano had proposed to her again. This time he'd got the proposal exactly right when she knew this was the only place she wanted to be, with her two favourite people in the world. For now he was working hard at the local emergency department and, despite her reservations, she was actually enjoying being a stay-at-home mum, though they had big plans for the future, setting up their own practice for the locals.

Today, getting married, with her mum and son in attendance, was the icing on the wedding cake.

'You haven't travelled in a year. I couldn't have you getting itchy feet.' He produced two tickets from his jacket pocket.

'It's not a cruise, is it?' She didn't really care where they were going as she hoped not to be leaving their bed for most of the trip, though as much as she loved their son, he had a habit of interrupting their nocturnal activities.

'Ugh. No. I'll never regret meeting you on board the ship, but I have had enough of those. I got us two first-class flights to the Seychelles instead.'

'What? Are you serious?'

'*Sì*. Just you, me and cocktails on the beach.'

'Sounds like paradise. Wait, what about Alessandro?' They couldn't just take off whenever they pleased when they had a baby who took priority over everything.

'Don't worry. You know my parents are dying to babysit and I'm dying to get you alone.'

The idea of spending quality time, preferably naked, with her new husband gave her the same thrill as the first night they'd succumbed to temptation.

'What are we waiting for, then? Let's go and get married.' She tucked the tickets safely back into his pocket and hooked her arm through his.

She couldn't wait to say her vows. Luciano was the only man she wanted to share her life and her dreams with. This time she knew it would be for ever.

* * * * *

*If you enjoyed this story, check
out these other great reads from
Karin Baine*

Reunion with His Surgeon Princess
Healed by Their Unexpected Family
Their One-Night Christmas Gift
Their One-Night Twin Surprise

All available now!